the Mountains of Majipoor

Books by Robert Silverberg

At Winter's End
The Book of Skulls
Born with the Dead
Downward to the Earth
Dying Inside
The Face of the Waters
Gilgamesh the King
Hot Sky at Midnight
Kingdoms of the Wall
Lord Valentine's Castle
Majipoor Chronicles
The Masks of Time
The Mountains of Majipoor
The New Springtime
Nightwings
Secret Sharers: The Collected Stories of Robert Silverberg, Volume I
Thorns
Valentine Pontifex
The World Inside

With Isaac Asimov

Nightfall
The Ugly Little Boy
The Positronic Man

BANTAM BOOKS
New York Toronto London
Sydney Auckland

The Mountains of Majipoor

Robert Silverberg

THE MOUNTAINS OF MAJIPOOR
A Bantam Book / March 1995

Book design by Maria Carella

Library of Congress Cataloging-in-Publication Data

Silverberg, Robert.
The mountains of Majipoor / Robert Silverberg.
p. cm.
ISBN 0-553-09614-1
I. Title.
PS3569.I472M68 1995
813'.54—dc20 94-28950
CIP

Published simultaneously in the United States and Canada

Bantam Books are published by Bantam Books, a division of Bantam Doubleday Dell Publishing Group, Inc. Its trademark, consisting of the words "Bantam Books" and the portrayal of a rooster, is Registered in U.S. Patent and Trademark Office and in other countries. Marca Registrada. Bantam Books, 1540 Broadway, New York, New York 10036.

PRINTED IN THE UNITED STATES OF AMERICA

FFG 0 9 8 7 6 5 4 3 2 1

For Lou Aronica

Editors and publishers may come and go,
but a friend is a friend forever.

"I can be bold to say, that no man will ever venture farther than I have done. . . . Thick fogs, Snow storms, Intense Cold and every other thing that can render Navigation dangerous one has to encounter and these difficulties are greatly heightned by the enexpressable horrid aspect of the Country, a Country doomed by Nature never once to feel the warmth of the Suns rays, but to lie for ever buried under everlasting snow and ice. . . ."

—Captain James Cook,
Journals

the Mountains of Majipoor

1

The sky, which had been a frosty blue all these weeks of Harpirias's northward journey into this bleak and turbulent land, was the color of lead today. The air had grown so cold that it seemed to burn the skin. And a fierce cutting wind had suddenly begun rushing down through the narrow pass in the great mountain wall just ahead, carrying with it clouds of tiny hard particles, myriad sharp-edged things that struck Harpirias's unprotected cheeks like little stinging insects.

"Prince, you asked me yesterday what a snowstorm was like," said Korinaam the Shapeshifter, who was the expedition's guide. "Today you'll find out."

"I thought it was supposed to be summer here just now," Harpirias said. "Does it snow in the Khyntor Marches even in summer?"

"Even in summer, oh, yes, it does that very often," Korinaam replied serenely. "Sometimes for many days on end. Wolf-summer, we call that. When the snowdrifts pile higher than a Skandar's head, and famished steetmoys come out of the far north by the dozens to prey on the herds of the farmers in the foothills."

"By the Lady, if that's summer, what can the winters in this place be like, then?"

"If you are a believing man, you would do well to pray that the Divine never gives you the opportunity to find out," said Korinaam. "Come, prince. The pass awaits us."

Harpirias squinted uneasily toward the fanged heights before them. The heavy sky looked bruised and swollen. With mounting vigor the churning wind threw maddening handfuls of those sharp little particles in his face.

Surely it was suicidal to be going up into the teeth of that storm. Scowling, Harpirias glanced toward Korinaam. The Shapeshifter seemed untroubled by the gathering fury above. His frail, attenuated figure was clad only in a twist of yellow cloth around his waist; his rubbery-looking greenish torso showed no reaction to the sudden bitter cold; his face, virtually featureless—tiny nose, slit of a mouth, narrow eyes sharply slanting beneath heavy hoods—was almost impossible to read.

"Do you really think it's wise to try to take the pass while it's snowing?" Harpirias asked.

"Wiser than to wait down here for the avalanches and the floods that will follow them," the Shapeshifter said. His eyehoods drew back for a moment. There was an uncompromising look in the dark implacable eyes beneath. "When traveling these roads in wolf-summer time, the higher the better is the rule, prince. Come. The real snowfall isn't upon us yet. This is only harbinger-ice, the vanguard that rides on the first wind. We ought to be moving onward before things get worse."

Korinaam jumped into the floater that he shared with Harpirias. Eight similar vehicles were lined up behind it along the narrow mountain road. Aboard them were the two dozen soldiers of this expedition to the inhospitable northlands which Harpirias so reluctantly found himself leading, and the equipment that was supposed to tide them through their difficult and dangerous venture into this desolate, forbidding country. But Harpirias hesitated a moment more, standing beside the open door of the floater, staring up in awe and wonder at the oncoming storm.

Snow! Actual snow!

He had heard of snow. He had read of it in storybooks when he was a child: frozen water, it was, water that had been turned by extreme cold to some kind of tangible substance. It sounded magical: lovely white dust, austere and pure, cold beyond all comprehension, that would melt at the touch of your finger.

Magical, yes. Unreal, the stuff of fable and witchcraft. Hardly anywhere on the whole vast world of Majipoor was it possible to encounter temperatures low enough actually to freeze water. Certainly one did not ever find snow on the airy slopes of Castle Mount, where Harpirias had spent his boyhood and young manhood among the knights and princes of the Coronal's court, and where the great weather-machines built in ancient times kept the Fifty Cities wrapped in eternal gentle springtime.

It was said that snow sometimes fell in the worst of winters along the highest ridges of certain other mountain peaks, though: atop Mount Zygnor in northern Alhanroel, and in the Gonghar range that ran across the midsection of the continent of Zimroel. But Harpirias had never been within a thousand miles of Zygnor, nor within five thousand of the Gonghars. He had never been anywhere at all where snow might be probable, until suddenly he was thrust into the command of this unlikely mission into Zimroel's far northland—into the harsh and lofty mountain-girt plateau known as the Khyntor Marches. The veritable motherland of snow, that was, infamous for its howling icy gales and formidable glacier-locked peaks. Here alone in all of Majipoor did true winter reign: behind the awesome mountains known as the Nine Sisters that cut an entire peninsula off from the rest of the world and doomed it to a stern frigid climate of its own.

But Harpirias and his companions were making their Khyntor journey in summer. And so even here he was not expecting to experience a snowfall, but only perhaps to catch a glimpse of the leftover snow of the winter before, lying along the rims of the topmost peaks. As indeed he had. The travelers were no more than a few hundred miles north of the green round-bosomed hills that rise behind the city of Ni-moya when the landscape had begun to change, lush dense shrubbery giving way to sparse stands of yellow-boled trees, and then they were in the foothills of the Marches, climbing steadily across a rising terrain of flat gray shields of granite cut by swift streams, and at last the first of the Nine Sisters of Khyntor came into sight: Threilikor, the Weeping Sister. But there was no snow on Threilikor in this season, only the multitude of streams and rivulets and cascades that gave her her name.

The next mountain they reached, though, was Javnikor, the Black Sister, and the road that took them past her flank showed Harpirias her north face, where near the summit the dark rock was brightly encrusted here and there with a scattering of white patches, like sinister encroaching blemishes. Still farther to the north, along the sides of the mountain known as Cuculimaive—the Lovely Sister, a symmetrical pile of pink stone festooned with uncountable rocky spires and parapets and outcroppings of all imaginable shapes—Harpirias beheld something even stranger, long grayish-white tongues of ice trailing down, which Korinaam said were glaciers. "Frozen rivers of ice is what they are, rivers of ice that flow down into the lowlands, slowly, very slowly, moving just a few feet every year."

Rivers of ice! How could there be such a thing?

And now before them lay the Twin Sisters, Shelvokor and

Malvokor, which could not be gone around but must be ascended if the travelers were to attain their destination. Two great square-shouldered blocks of stone side by side, they were, immensely broad and so high that Harpirias could not begin to guess their height, and their upper reaches were mantled thickly in white, even on their south faces, so that when the sun struck their surfaces they were blinding to behold. A single narrow pass led up and between them, which Korinaam said must now be traversed. And down from that pass, scouring everything in its path, there blew a wind such as Harpirias had never felt before, a wind out of the Pit, a wolf-wind, a demon-wind, cold and biting and angry, carrying with it the sharp icy harbingers of a summer snowstorm.

"Well?" Korinaam said.

"You really think we should go up into that?"

"There is no other choice."

Harpirias shrugged and clambered into the floater next to the Shapeshifter. Korinaam touched the controls and the vehicle glided forward. The other floaters followed.

For a time the ascent merely seemed strange and beautiful. The snow came upon them in luminous wind-whipped ribbons that swirled and gusted in a wild frantic dance. The air before them took on a wondrous shimmer from the glittering flecks that were tossing about in it. A soft white cloak began to cover the black walls of the pass.

But after a time the storm intensified, the cloak wrapped

itself closer and closer about them. Harpirias could see nothing but whiteness, before, behind, above, to the right and left. On every side there was snow, only snow, a dense swaddling of snow.

Where was the road? It was miraculous that Korinaam was able to see it at all, let alone to follow every twist and turn.

Though it was warm enough inside the floater, Harpirias found himself starting to shiver and could not stop. From such glimpses of the pass as he had had in the early stages of the climb, he knew that the road was a treacherous one, switching back from side to side above terrible abysses as it rose between the two stolid mountains. Even if Korinaam did not simply steer the floater over the edge on one of the sharper turns, the wind was only too likely to pick the vehicle up and send it crashing down the slope.

Harpirias sat still, saying nothing, fighting to keep his teeth from chattering. It was not proper for him to show fear. He was a knight of the Coronal's court, a beneficiary of the severe and rigorous training that such a phrase implied. Nor was his ancestry that of a coward. A thousand years before, his celebrated ancestor Prestimion had ruled this world in glory, doing deeds of high renown, first as Coronal, then as Pontifex. Could a descendant of the resplendent Prestimion permit himself to display cowardice before a Shapeshifter?

No. No.

And yet—that driving wind—these curves—those blinding surges of ever-thickening snow—

Calmly Korinaam said, turning casually toward Harpirias as he spoke, "They tell the tale of the great beast Naamaaliilaa, who walked these mountains alone, in the days when she was the only being that lived on this world. And in a storm like this she breathed upon a cliff of ice, and licked with her tongue the place she had breathed on, and as her tongue moved, she carved a figure from it, and he was Saabaataan, the Blind Giant, the first man of our kind. And then she breathed again and licked again, and brought forth from the ice Siifiinaatuur, the Red Woman, the mother of us all. And Saabaataan and Siifiinaatuur went down out of this icy land into the forests of Zimroel, and were fruitful and multiplied and spread over all the world, and thus the race of Piurivars came into being. So this is a holy land to us, prince. In this place of frost and storm our first parents were conceived."

Harpirias responded only with a grunt. His interest in Shapeshifter creation myths was no more than moderate at the best of times, and this was something less than the best of times.

The wind struck the floater with the force of a giant fist. The vehicle lurched wildly, bobbing like a straw in the breeze and veering toward the brink of the abyss. Coolly Korinaam set it back on its course with the lightest touch of one long many-jointed finger.

Harpirias said through clenched teeth, "How much farther is it, would you say, to the valley of the Othinor?"

"Two passes and three valleys beyond this one, that's all."

"Ah. And how long will that take us, do you think?"

Korinaam smiled indifferently. "A week, maybe. Or two, or three. Or perhaps forever."

2

It had never been part of Harpirias's plan to go venturing into the dismal snowy wastes of the Khyntor Marches. As a member of one of the great pontifical families, a Prestimion of Muldemar, he had quite reasonably expected that he would pass his days comfortably on Castle Mount in the service of the Coronal Lord Ambinole, perhaps rising in time to the rank of counselor to the Coronal, or possibly some high ministry, or even the dukedom of one of the Fifty Cities.

But his upward path had been abruptly interrupted, and for the most cruel and trivial of reasons.

With a band of six companions he had ridden out from the Castle, on his twenty-fifth birthday, a fateful day for him, and down into the forested estate country close by the city of Halanx. His friend Tembidat's family long had maintained a hunting preserve there. The outing was Tembidat's idea, Tembidat's gift to him.

Hunting was one of Harpirias's greatest pleasures. He was

a man of short stature, like most of the men of the Prestimion line, but agile and broad-shouldered and strong, a genial, outgoing, athletic young man. He loved the chase in its every part: the stalking, the sighting of the prey, the sweet air whistling past his cheeks as he gave pursuit, the moment of pausing to take aim. And then, of course, the kill. What finer way to celebrate one's birthday than by slaughtering a few bilantoons or fierce-tusked tuamiroks in an elegant and skillful manner, and bringing the meat back for a joyous feast, and taking a trophy or two to hang on the wall?

All that day had Harpirias and his friends hunted, and with the greatest of success, bagging not only a score of bilantoons and a brace of tuamiroks but a fat succulent vandar as well, and a dainty high-prancing onathil, and, as the afternoon was waning, the most wondrous catch of all, a majestic sinileese that had a splendid glistening white hide and glorious many-branched scarlet antlers. Harpirias himself was the one to bring it down, with a single well-placed shot at an astonishing range, a clean shot that filled him with pride at his own marksmanship.

"I had no idea your family kept such rare creatures as this in its park," Harpirias said to Tembidat, when they had recovered the body of the sinileese and he was preparing it for transport back to the Castle.

"In fact I had no idea of it myself," said Tembidat in an oddly somber and uneasy tone, which might have served

Harpirias as a hint of what was to come. But Harpirias was too swollen with delight at his achievement to notice. "I confess I felt just a bit of surprise when I saw it standing there," Tembidat continued. "Rare indeed, a white sinileese—I've never seen a white sinileese before, have you?—"

"Perhaps I should have let it be," Harpirias said. "It may be some special prize of your father's—some particular favorite of his—"

"Of which he's never spoken? No, Harpirias!" Tembidat shook his head, a little too vigorously, perhaps, as though trying to convince himself of something. "He must not have known of it, or cared, or it wouldn't have been roaming loose. This is our family estate, and all animals here are fair game. And so the sinileese is my birthday present to you. My father would feel only joy, knowing that you were the one who had slain it, and that this is your birthday hunt."

"Who are those men, Tembidat?" asked one of the others in the hunting party suddenly. "Your father's gamekeepers, are they?"

Harpirias looked up. Three burly grim-faced strangers in crimson-and-purple livery had stepped from the forest into the clearing where the hunters were at work.

"No," said Tembidat, and that curious tautness had returned to his voice, "not my father's keepers, but those of our neighbor Prince Lubovine."

"Your—neighbor—" said Harpirias, with apprehension

growing in him as he considered the ample distance at which he had killed the sinileese.

He began to wonder, now, just whose beast the sinileese had been.

The biggest and most grim-looking of the crimson-and-purple strangers offered a careless salute and said, "Have any of you gentlemen happened to see— Ah, yes, apparently you have—"

His voice trailed off into a growl.

"A white sinileese with scarlet antlers," another of the newcomers finished tersely for him.

There was an ugly moment of hostile silence. The three were peering in a dark-visaged fashion at the animal over which Harpirias was crouching. Harpirias, putting down his skinning knife, stared at his bloodied hands. He felt a rushing roar in his ears, as of a seething torrent passing through his skull.

Tembidat said finally, with an unsteady touch of defiance in his tone, "You surely must know that this is the hunting preserve of the family of Duke Kestir of Halanx, whose son I am. If your animal strayed across the boundary onto our land, we regret its death, but we were completely within our rights to regard it as legitimate prey. As you well know."

"If it had strayed across," said the first of Prince Lubovine's gamekeepers. "If. But the sinileese, which we have been pursuing all afternoon since it broke from its cage, was on our prince's domain when you shot it."

"Your—prince's—domain—" Tembidat said, faltering.

"Indeed. Can you see the boundary marker over there, blazed on that pingla tree? The blood of the sinileese stains the ground well behind it. We have followed that bloody trail to here. You can carry the animal over the line to Duke Kestir's land, if you wish, but that does not change the fact that it was standing in Prince Lubovine's domain when you shot it."

"Is this true?" Harpirias said to Tembidat, with an edge of horror sharpening his words. "Is that the boundary of your father's land?"

"Apparently so," Tembidat muttered hollowly.

"And the animal was the only one of its kind, the grandest treasure of Prince Lubovine's collection," the gamekeeper said. "We claim its meat and its hide; but your foolish poaching will cost you much more than that, mark my words, my young princes."

The three wardens hoisted the sinileese to their shoulders, and stalked off into the forest with it.

Harpirias stood stunned. Prince Lubovine's park of rare beasts was legendary for the marvels it contained. And Prince Lubovine was not only a man of great power and immeasurable wealth and high ancestry—he traced his lineage back to the

Coronal Lord Voriax, elder brother of the famous Valentine, who had been Coronal and then Pontifex during the Time of Troubles five centuries before—but also he was known as a man of petty and vindictive nature, who brooked no affront lightly.

How could Tembidat have been so stupid as to let the hunting party wander right up to the border of Lubovine's estate? Why had Tembidat not said that the boundary was unfenced, why had he not warned him how risky it might be to aim at that far-off sinileese?

Tembidat, plainly aware of Harpirias's dismay, said gently, "We will make full amends, my friend, have no doubt of that. My father will speak to Lubovine—we will make it clear that it was simply a mistake, that you had not the slightest intent of poaching—we will buy him three new sinileeses, *five* new sinileeses—"

But of course it wasn't as simply dealt with as that.

There were profound apologies. There was the payment of an indemnity. There was an attempt—fruitless—to find another white sinileese for the outraged Prince Lubovine. Highly placed kinsmen of Harpirias's, Prestimions and Dekkerets and Kinnikens, spoke on his behalf, urging leniency for what had been, after all, an innocent youthful error.

And then, just when he thought the whole affair had blown over, Harpirias found himself transferred to an obscure diplomatic post in the giant city of Ni-moya, on Majipoor's subsidiary continent of Zimroel, far across the sea, thousands and thousands of miles from Castle Mount.

The decree crashed down upon him like the falling of an axe. In effect, his career was over. Once he had gone to Zimroel he would be forgotten at the Castle. He might be gone for years, even decades; he might never win reassignment to the governmental center. And his duties in Ni-moya would be meaningless; he would spend his days shuffling papers, filing trifling reports, and stamping his seal on pointless documents, year after year; and meanwhile all the other young lordlings of his generation would vault past him to the high posts of the Coronal's court that should have been his by right of birth and ability.

"This is Lubovine's doing, isn't it?" Harpirias asked Tembidat when it was clear that the transfer was irrevocable. "This is how he's taking his revenge for that damned sinileese of his. But it isn't fair—to ruin a man's entire life simply because a stupid animal got killed by accident—"

"Your life won't be ruined, Harpirias."

"Won't it?"

"You'll spend six months in Ni-moya, a year at most. My father is certain of it. Lubovine is very powerful and he insists on extracting one final squeeze of retribution from you for what you did, so you'll have to serve a kind of penitential exile out there for a little while, and then you'll be back. The Coronal has assured him of that."

"And you believe it'll really happen that way?"

"Absolutely," said Tembidat.

But that was, however, not the way things worked out.

Off went Harpirias to Ni-moya with the darkest forebodings. It was, at any rate, a grand and beautiful city, the greatest one in Zimroel, a place of more than thirty million inhabitants, hundreds of miles of wonderful white towers rising above the swift waters of the mighty River Zimr. But it was a city of Zimroel, all the same. No one who has been raised amid the splendors of Castle Mount can adapt lightly to the lesser glories of the other continent.

And there in Ni-moya Harpirias remained for one dreary month after another, performing negligible and insulting bureaucratic functions in something called the Office of Provincial Liaison, which seemed to fall neither into the sphere of the Coronal nor that of the Pontifex but into a kind of governmental limbo somewhere between.

He waited eagerly for the message summoning him back to Castle Mount. And waited.

And waited.

Several times he filed formal application for a transfer to duty at the Mount. He received no answers. He wrote to Tembidat, reminding him of the Coronal's alleged promise to let him come home after a while. Tembidat replied that he was completely convinced that the Coronal intended to make good on his word.

The anniversary of Harpirias's arrival came and went, and he began a second year of exile.

By now Harpirias was getting only the sketchiest of news from his friends and kinsmen at the Castle: an occasional brief letter, stray bits of gossip, greater and greater spaces between each communication. It was as if they were becoming embarrassed to write to him. So everything was happening just as he had feared. He was forgotten. His career was at an end; he would finish his days as a minor bureaucrat in this obscure administrative department in this prodigiously big but distinctly provincial city of Majipoor's secondary continent, forever cut off from the sources of power and privilege to which he had had access all the years of his life.

His soul itself began to change. He who had been so rollicking and outgoing turned crabbed and harsh and inward, a sullen man, embittered perhaps beyond all soothing by the wrong that had been done to him.

Then one day when Harpirias was going through the newly arrived diplomatic pouch from Alhanroel, picking spiritlessly over the latest miscellany of empty documents with which he would be expected to deal, he was startled to come upon one that was addressed personally to him—an envelope that bore the insignia of Prince Salteir, High Counselor to the Coronal Lord Ambinole.

Harpirias had never expected to receive anything from so notable a figure as Salteir again. With trembling fingers he broke the seal. And began to read in wonder and delight.

A transfer! Lubovine had relented! They were lifting him out of Ni-moya at last!

But, as he continued to read, his brief flare of exultation turned swiftly to ashes. Instead of being called back to the center of government, he was being sent even farther away. Hadn't burying him in Ni-moya been sufficient vengeance for Lubovine? Apparently not. For now, to his deep chagrin and utter dismay, Harpirias discovered that his newest assignment would send him beyond the boundaries of civilization itself: into the forlorn, ice-bound mountainous territories of Zimroel's far northeastern region, the Khyntor Marches.

3

What had happened, Harpirias was to learn, was that a scientific expedition had ventured into the cheerless and virtually uninhabited realm that was the Marches in search of the supposed fossil remains of certain extinct land-dwelling dragons: gigantic reptilian creatures of an earlier era, related in some fashion to the immense and intelligent sea-dragons that to this day still wandered the immeasurable oceans of Majipoor in swarming herds.

Confused and contradictory tales of the one-time existence of such land-dragons on Majipoor were common to the mythology of many of the races that inhabited the giant planet. Among the Liimen, that unfortunate race of poor and itinerant sausage-sellers and fishermen, it was an article of faith that in a former epoch the dragons had lived upon the land, then had chosen to retreat to the sea, and would at some apocalyptic time take up residence on shore once again and bring about the salvation of the world. The Hjorts and the shaggy four-armed Skandars embraced similar beliefs; and the Shapeshifters or

Metamorphs, the true aborigines of the planet, apparently had some such notions of their own, involving a long-vanished golden age when they and the dragons had been the only inhabitants of Majipoor, the two races living in telepathic harmony both on the land and in the sea. But it was difficult for anyone who was not himself a Metamorph to know what it was that the Metamorphs really believed.

The documents that Harpirias received told him that a party of steetmoy-hunters, roving unusually far to the north one mild summer, had penetrated deep into the normally snowy reaches of the Khyntor Marches and had spied outcroppings of fossilized bones of titanic size jutting from a barren rock formation high up near the rim of a remote canyon.

On the supposition that the bones were those of the legendary land-dragons, a party of some eight or ten paleontologists had received permission from the administrative authorities in Zimroel to go in search of the fossil outcropping. A Metamorph named Korinaam—a native of Ni-moya who, like a number of his people, had long earned his living by leading hunting parties into the more accessible regions of the Arctic zone—was hired to convey them into the Marches.

"They went up there early last summer," said Heptil Magloir, the little Vroon from the Bureau of Antiquities who had signed the original exploration permit. "Nothing was heard from them for months. Then, in late fall, just before the full onset of the snowy season in the Marches, Korinaam returned to Ni-moya. Alone. The entire scientific party had been captured and was being held prisoner, he said, and he had been sent back to negotiate terms for their release."

Harpirias raised his eyebrows. "Prisoners? Prisoners of whom? Surely not the March-men." Tribes of rugged half-civilized nomads were known to roam the Marches, descending once in a while into the settled regions of Zimroel to offer furs and leather for sale, and the meat of the northland beasts they hunted. But these mountain folk, wild as they sometimes seemed, had never sought to raise any challenge against the vastly more numerous and powerful city-dwelling people of Majipoor.

"Not March-men, no," said the Vroon, who was a many-tentacled creature barely higher than Harpirias's knee. "At least, none that we have ever had dealings with before. It seems that the explorers were seized by a race of fierce barbarians—a people previously unknown to us, native to the northern Marches."

"A lost race?" said Harpirias, suddenly fascinated. "Some isolated bunch of Shapeshifters, do you mean?"

"Humans. The backward descendants, so Korinaam says, of a small band of fur traders who went off into the upper Marches thousands of years ago and became trapped—or chose to trap themselves—in a little ice-bound valley, which until the recent spate of relatively warm years was completely cut off from the rest of Majipoor. They've devolved into the ugliest kind of savagery, and know nothing of the outside world. For example, they don't have the slightest inkling that Majipoor is a planet of inconceivable size which contains billions of people. They believe that the whole world is pretty much like their own region, inhabited by a few scattered tribes of primitives who live by hunting and foraging. And when they were told about the Coronal and the Pontifex, they evidently understood them to be nothing more than petty tribal chieftains."

"Why take the scientists prisoner, though?"

"The main concern of these people, if I can dignify them with that term," answered the Vroon, "is simply to be left alone. They want to be allowed to go on living as they've always lived, safe from intrusion up there in the age-old isolation of their little valley, behind its wall of snow and ice. They've demanded a guarantee of that from the Coronal. And they intend to keep our paleontologists as hostages until we come across with a treaty to that effect."

Harpirias nodded gloomily. "So I've been picked to serve as our ambassador to this bunch of mountain savages, is that it?"

"Exactly so."

"Wonderful. And I suppose I'm to go to them and tell them sweetly and kindly—assuming that I can communicate with them at all—that the Coronal deplores this shameful violation of their privacy and respects their sacred territorial rights, and he pledges that no attempts will be made to send settlers into the unappealing icebox where they prefer to live. And I'm to let them know that as the authorized representative of His Majesty Lord Ambinole I am fully empowered to sign the treaty promising everything they are asking. In return for all this they are to release the hostages forthwith. Do I have it right?"

"There is one little complication," said Heptil Magloir.

"Only one?"

"They aren't expecting an ambassador. They expect the Coronal himself to come."

Harpirias gasped. "But they can't really think he will!"

"Unfortunately, they do. As I've already told you, they have no comprehension whatever of the size of Majipoor, or of the grandeur and majesty of the Coronal, or of the high responsibilities over which he presides. And these mountaineers are proud and touchy people. Their domain has been trespassed upon by strangers, which is apparently something they don't permit; it strikes them as perfectly right and proper that those strangers' chieftain now should show up in their village and humbly beg their pardon."

"I see," said Harpirias. "And therefore you want me to go to them and abjectly prostrate myself before them, all the while pretending that I'm Lord Ambinole. Is that it?"

The Vroon's multitude of ropy tentacles moved in an agitated way. Softly he said, "No such statement was made by me."

"Well, who am I supposed to be, then?"

"Be anybody that will make them happy. Tell them anything at all, so long as it gets those scientists free."

"Anything. Up to and including masquerading as the Coronal?"

"The tactics you employ are for you to choose," said Heptil Magloir primly. "These matters are entirely up to your discretion. You have a completely free hand. A man of your skill and tact will undoubtedly be equal to the task."

"Yes. Undoubtedly."

Harpirias took a few deep breaths. They wanted him to lie. They would not *tell* him to lie, but they had no objections to it, if lying to the savages was what it took to free the hostages. That saddened and angered him. Though Harpirias was far from straitlaced, the idea of posing as the Coronal among these barbarians seemed shockingly improper to him. It was offensive that they would even suggest it. What sort of man did they think he was?

Crisply he said, after a bit, "And when, may I ask, am I supposed to set out on this embassy?"

"At the beginning of the Khyntor summer. It's the only time of year when the region where these people live is even slightly accessible."

"That gives me some months yet."

"So it does."

This all was like some very bad joke. The thought of undertaking this crazy chase off into the frigid Arctic wilderness filled Harpirias with despair.

"And if I were to decline the assignment?" he asked, after another brief pause.

"Decline? Decline?" The Vroon repeated the word as though he scarcely understood its meaning.

"I have no experience, after all, with travel under such difficult conditions."

"The Metamorph Korinaam will be your guide."

"Of course," Harpirias said dourly. "That should make it all much easier."

The question of his refusing to undertake the mission seemed to have been brushed aside. Harpirias suspected that it would not be useful to raise it again.

But his doom was sealed, he knew, if he actually did let himself be sent off into the snowy wastes of the Marches. The journey would not be a quick or easy one, and the negotiations with those proud barbarians were bound to be maddeningly lengthy and frustrating. By the time he returned from the northlands—if ever he did—he would beyond any doubt have spent too much time in obscure parts of the world to have any hope of reclaiming his old position at Lord Ambinole's court. The other young men of his group would have gobbled up all the really important posts. The best he could hope for was to be a petty bureaucrat for the rest of his life; but more probably he would die in the course of this absurd and hazardous expedition, perhaps lost in some great snowstorm or else slain out of hand by the brutal mountaineers when they came to realize that he was not the Coronal, only some minor functionary of the diplomatic service.

All this, for one white sinileese! Oh, Lubovine, Lubovine, what have you done to me?

Perhaps there was some way he could get out of this, though. The long winter of the Marches still had some while to run, which gave Harpirias a little time to maneuver before he was supposed to depart. Cautiously he consulted a few of his senior colleagues at the Office of Provincial Liaison about the necessity of his accepting this new assignment.

Was there any appeal mechanism in the department by which he could claim the urgency of his present work as a reason for refusing the embassy to the Marches? They peered at him as though he were speaking some alien language. Could he decline on grounds of jeopardy to his health? They shrugged. What effect would it have on his career if he turned the assignment down? Nothing other than catastrophic, they replied.

He debated throwing himself upon the mercy of Prince Lubovine. But that would be idiotic, he decided.

He considered appealing to the Coronal himself. No, it was probably very unwise to try that: one did not want to define oneself before Lord Ambinole as a person who shrank from uncomfortable duties, after all. And as for going over the Coronal's head to the senior monarch of the realm, the Pontifex Taghin Gawad cloistered deep in his imperial Labyrinth, why, that would be true madness, futile beyond words.

What he did do was to compose eloquent despondent letters to his highly placed kinsmen at court; but he left them in his files, unsent.

The weeks ticked by. In Ni-moya, where the weather was always mild and warm, the daylight hours now stretched far into the evening. Summer, or whatever passed for summer in that place, must be at last on its way to the Khyntor Marches, Harpirias realized dolefully. The northlands expedition was rolling toward him like an avalanche and there evidently was no way of shunting it aside.

"A visitor for you," his aide announced one morning.

A visitor? A visitor? No one ever came visiting him here! Who—

"Tembidat!" Harpirias cried, as a long-legged young man in the gaudy finery of a Castle lordling came striding into his office. "What are you doing in Ni-moya?"

"A little business on behalf of my family," Tembidat said. "We have stajja plantations not very far west of here that have been badly mismanaged in recent years, it seems. So I talked my father into letting me make an inspection tour and set things to rights. With a side trip to Ni-moya to see a certain old friend." He glanced around, shaking his head. "So this is where you work?"

"Magnificent, isn't it?"

"If only I could tell you how sorry I am that any of this had to happen, Harpirias—how hard I've worked to get you out of this mess—" Tembidat's expression brightened. "But it's almost over now. Another few weeks and you can kiss this ghastly place goodbye, isn't that so, old man?"

"You know about my new mission?"

"Know about it? I helped to arrange it!"

"You *what?*"

"Oh, it was mostly your cousin Vildimuir who set things up for you," Tembidat said, grinning broadly. "He was the first to hear the story about those nitwit scientists who got themselves captured by the wild men of the mountains, and he started in right away among the Coronal's men, angling for you to be placed in charge of the rescue mission. Then he told me about it, and I put a word in for you with the Ministry of Frontier Affairs, which as you might expect is terribly excited about the whole thing because there's a newly discovered primitive culture involved that's going to require special handling, and that might just lead to a bigger budget for the Ministry; and I managed to convince none other than Inamon Ghaznavis that you were absolutely the best man to go up there and talk to them, in view of your diplomatic background and the fact that you were stationed here in Ni-moya anyway, just a hop and a skip from the foothills of the Marches, and so—"

"Wait a minute," Harpirias broke in. "I can't believe what

you're saying. Isn't it bad enough that I've been dumped into this miserable dead-end job here? Did you and Vildimuir think it was going to make things any better for me by entangling me in some crazy expedition into a horrendous frostbitten place where no civilized man has ever gone before?"

"Absolutely."

"How so?"

Tembidat glared at him as though he were thick-witted.

"Listen to me, Harpirias," he said. "This expedition is the only chance you have to save yourself from having to spend the rest of your days pushing moronic government papers around in this office."

"The Coronal, so you once swore to me, was going to pardon me after a few months and let me come back to—"

"*Listen* to me," said Tembidat. "The Coronal has forgotten all about you. Don't you think he's got other things on his mind? The only bit of information he's likely to remember about Harpirias of Muldemar is that he did something once that got Prince Lubovine very angry, and Lubovine can be such a pain in the neck that the Coronal doesn't want to stir him up again over whatever it is that you did, so whenever one of us brings up the subject of recalling you to Castle Mount he just brushes it aside. And after a time he won't even remember who you were or why there's any reason to reinstate you at the Castle. All right. Now you get sent off into the Marches to rescue a bunch of lost scientists from a lost tribe of ferocious savages. No doubt your journey is going to be extremely harrowing and grueling and you'll be called upon to perform all sorts of grand heroic deeds along the way."

"No doubt," Harpirias said blackly.

"There's no question of it. Be serious, Harpirias."

"I'm trying to be," Harpirias said. "It's not easy."

He was surprised himself at how sharp and cynical and suspicious he had become, here in Ni-moya. The Harpirias of Castle Mount had been nothing at all like that. There were times these days that he could hardly recognize himself, so thoroughly had he changed.

Tembidat went on undaunted. "So your trip will be a glorious epic endeavor. You'll go to the northlands, perform bravely and well under highly difficult circumstances, and make your way safely back through all the perils, bringing the hostages with you. In all probability the Coronal, who is easily stirred by tales of great exploits and high adventure that seem to hearken back to some more romantic era, is going to want to hear all about your experiences. So you'll be called back to the Castle to deliver your report in person, and Lord Ambinole will be tremendously delighted by your stirring account of heroic thrills and chills on the ice-fields of the north, Harpirias, *tremendously* delighted, and by the vivid descriptions you'll give him of your death-defying rescue of those brilliant scientists, a deed which is going to be celebrated for centuries to come in song and story. And of *course* he's not going to ship you back to some stupid desk job in Ni-moya after he's heard all that."

"Of course. Unless I don't happen to survive this glorious epic adventure in the first place, that is. Unless it turns out that I get clobbered by an avalanche or wind up being eaten by the savages."

"If you want to be a hero of song and story, Harpirias, you have to take a few risks. But there's no reason in the world why you shouldn't—"

"Can't you understand, Tembidat, I *don't* want to be a hero of song and story? I just want to get out of this dreadful place and back to the Mount, where I belong."

"Very well. This is the only way to achieve that."

"It's a lunatic thing to do," said Harpirias. "The risks are overwhelmingly great and the possibility of any kind of real payoff for me is merely hypothetical."

"I agree."

"Then how can you expect me to be willing to—"

Tembidat sighed. "There's simply no alternative, Harpirias. This is the one and only opportunity you're going to get. Look here: your distinguished cousin Vildimuir has gone pretty far out on a limb to get you this assignment. It meant crossing departmental lines and pulling strings at three or four Ministries, while at the same time keeping various other people who actually wanted command of this expedition from getting it.

I'm talking about our old friends Sinnim and Graniwain and Noridath, specifically. They thought a little jaunt into the Marches might be *fun.* Do you remember the concept of fun, Harpirias? Seeing strange scenery, making your way through a dangerous unknown place, coping with a savage warlike race: they were more than eager to go, let me tell you, and they weren't the only ones. With extreme difficulty Vildimuir succeeded in snaring the assignment for you instead. If you embarrass him now by turning the job down, you can bet that he isn't going to knock himself out finding you some other way out of Ni-moya, do you follow me? Either you go, Harpirias, or you settle down here for keeps and learn to love the work that you're doing right now. Those are your only choices."

"I see. What an extremely pretty situation." Harpirias turned away to keep Tembidat from seeing the anguish in his eyes. "So everything really is over for me, isn't it? All because I fired a single shot at a silly animal with fancy red antlers."

"Don't be such a pessimist, old man. What's happened to you? Where's your sense of adventure? You'll make the trip, you'll achieve everything you're supposed to, and you'll come home a hero and start your career all over again. Jump for it, Harpirias! How many chances for excitement like this does any of us get in a lifetime? I'd be happy to go with you myself, if I could."

"Would you? What's stopping you?"

Color came to Tembidat's face. "I'm here on complicated

family business that's going to take me months to clean up, or I would. You know very well that I would. But never mind, Harpirias. Turn the assignment down, if that's how you feel. I'll tell Vildimuir that you were deeply grateful for all his help, but that in the end you decided that you really preferred your nice quiet desk job in Ni-moya, and therefore—"

"Don't be an imbecile, Tembidat. Of course I'm going to go."

"You are?"

Harpirias managed a smile. The effort was considerable. "Did you ever seriously think I wouldn't?"

4

The storm went on and on, hour after hour. After a time, Harpirias came to take it for granted that the world should consist of nothing but whiteness. That other world in which he had once lived, the world of colors, of green trees and red flowers and blue rivers and turquoise sky, seemed now to have been only a dream. What was real was the insistent swarms of small white particles that came endlessly hurtling against the front screen of the floater on the tireless driving gusts of wind, and the thick mantle of whiteness that wrapped it snugly on every side, above and below, before and behind, blurring everything into indistinguishability.

He said nothing. Asked no questions, offered no comments. He sat impassively, like a figure of wood, while Korinaam beside him steered the floater with almost arrogant confidence through the horrific gale.

How long did these wolf-summer storms last? How far was it to the other side of the pass? How many of the other floaters were still following along behind them? Harpirias's mind brimmed with questions of this sort; but they rose like flotsam on the tide, and bobbed about a moment, and were quickly gone again. The unrelenting snow was almost hypnotic. It lulled him into a calm waking sleep, a pleasant numbness of the soul.

Gradually the fury of the storm gave over. The air cleared. The onslaught of rushing ice-particles ceased to assail them and only a few spiraling flakes now drifted down. The wall of cloud overhead grew frayed and tattered, and broke, and the sun reappeared, golden-green, magnificent. Distinct shapes began to take form out of the universal furry whiteness: the black fangs of rocky cliffs rearing up beside the roadway, the tormented angularity of some giant tree thrusting almost horizontally from the side of the mountain wall, the iron mass of a cloud against the paler background of the sky. The drifting heaps of gleaming powdery snow were already beginning to melt.

Harpirias, emerging from his trance, saw that the road was wider here, and that it was descending at a gentle but steady slope. The view was clear ahead. They had traversed the pass between the two blocky mountains and were entering into an open place of sparse long-stalked grass and bare granite boulders, a broad apron-shaped plateau that stretched far into the grayish distance, with other mountains beyond.

He looked around. The second floater was riding practically on their heels and others were visible farther back.

"How many do you see?" Korinaam asked.

Harpirias shaded his eyes as he stared into the sun-blink that had followed the snow, and counted the vehicles as they came down the last curvetting switchback out of the pass. "Six—seven—eight."

"Good. No need to wait for anybody, then."

It amazed Harpirias that the entire convoy had been able to get safely across the precarious pass in that blinding storm. But everyone back in Ni-moya had assured him that his little army was made up of capable troops. There were about two dozen soldiers in all; he was the only human. Nearly all the members of his expeditionary force were towering brawny Skandars, ponderous furry four-armed people of great strength and superb coordination, whose ancestors had come to Majipoor long ago from some world where snow and cold must have been nothing at all unusual. Harpirias had a few Ghayrogs under his command as well, sleek-scaled green-eyed folk whose aspect was reptilian, with flickering forked tongues and writhing snaky coils sprouting from their heads, though in fact they were mammalian enough internally in most respects.

That seemed to Harpirias like a very skimpy force indeed to go up against an entire tribe of belligerent barbarians on their home grounds. But Korinaam had insisted that to bring more troops would be a grave error: "The mountain passes are extremely difficult ones. You would have a very hard time conveying a large party through them. Besides, the mountain people themselves would look upon any sizable army as an invasion force rather than a diplomatic mission. Almost certainly they would attack you from ambush, striking from strategic points high above the passes. Against such guerrilla warfare," the Shapeshifter argued, "you would have no chance whatever."

Now that he had seen the first of the passes through which they must go, Harpirias realized that Korinaam had been right. Even without the added complication of a snowstorm such as this one, there was no way they could defend themselves against attack by the mountaineers. Best to give the appearance of coming in peace, and depend on the good will of the tribesmen, such as it might be, than to offer the pretense of significant might, when in fact any show of strength by an army of outlanders would be unsustainable in these easily defended heights.

The summer sun, high and powerful now, swiftly consumed the freshly fallen snow. White drifts and spires turned quickly to soft slush and then became brooks of fast-moving runoff; enormous fluffy masses clinging to high rock faces broke free and came gliding down to land in silent billowy explosions; deep puddles sprang up almost instantaneously; the roadbed turned to a sticky wallow, over which the floaters hovered in fastidious disdain, rising an extra two or three feet from ground level to avoid stirring up muddy eddies. The air grew strangely bright, with a hard crystalline edge on it not seen in lower latitudes. Birds of the most splendid hues, with plumages of blazing scarlet and incandescent green and deep, radiant blue, came forth in sudden innumerable multitudes and swarmed overhead like throngs of lovely insects. It was almost impossible to believe that only an hour earlier a terrible snow-storm had been raging here.

"Look there," Korinaam said. "Haiguses. Coming out to hunt for stragglers after the storm. Nasty things, they are."

Harpirias followed the Metamorph's pointing arm. Some twenty or thirty small thick-furred animals had popped out of caves halfway up the rock slopes bordering the valley and were scuttering quickly down from boulder to boulder, moving with an awesome agility. Most had reddish fur, a few were black. All had large gleaming eyes, a furious blood-red crimson in color, and each was armed with a trio of long needle-sharp horns that splayed out menacingly at wide angles from its flat broad forehead.

They moved as a pack, surrounding smaller animals and hounding them out into the open, where they were speared and quickly devoured. Harpirias shuddered. Their efficiency and insatiability were impressive and frightening.

"They'll attack you or me the same way," said Korinaam. "Eight or ten of them can bring down even a Skandar. Leap straight up like fleas, gore him in the belly, swarm all over him. The March-men hunt them for their fur. Mainly the black ones, which are rarer than the red, and prized accordingly."

"I would think they'd be a lot rarer, if they're the only ones that get hunted."

"A black haigus isn't all that easy to catch. They're smarter and faster than the red ones, too: a superior breed in every way. You'll see only the great hunters wearing black haigus robes. And the king of the Othinor, naturally."

"Then I should be wearing black haigus too," said Harpirias. "To show him how important I am. A stole, at the very minimum, if not a full robe. I have some skill at hunting, you see, and—"

"Leave the haiguses for the haigus-hunters, my friend. They know how to deal with them. You don't want to go anywhere near those foul little animals, no matter how much of a hunter you may be. A safer way of showing King Toikella how important you are would be by conducting yourself before him with true kingly presence and majesty—as though you are a Coronal."

"As though," said Harpirias. "Well, why not? I can do that. There's already been one Coronal in my family, after all."

"Has there, now?" Korinaam asked, without much interest.

"Prestimion. Coronal to the great Pontifex Confalume. When he became Pontifex himself, his Coronal was Lord Dekkeret. More than a thousand years ago, this was."

"Indeed," said Korinaam. "My knowledge of your race's history is a little vague. But if you have a Coronal's blood in your veins, well, then, you should be capable of comporting yourself like one."

"Like one, perhaps. But not *as* one."

"What do you mean?"

"The Vroon from the Department of Antiquities who gave me this job—Heptil Magloir, that was his name—suggested that things would go easier for me up here if I told the Othinor that I actually *was* the Coronal."

"He did, did he?" Korinaam chuckled. "In truth it wouldn't actually be such a bad idea. The Coronal is the person they're expecting, you know. You do know that, don't you?"

"Yes, I do. But I'm under no formal instructions to pretend that I'm Lord Ambinole. Nor am I going to do any such thing."

"Even for the sake of easing the negotiations?"

"Even," said Harpirias sharply. "It's entirely out of the question."

"Well then, prince," Korinaam said, with a hint of amusement or perhaps mockery in his inflection. "It's out of the question, I suppose. If you say so."

"I say so, yes."

The Shapeshifter laughed quietly again. Harpirias felt a burst of irritation at being condescended to this way. How very much like a Shapeshifter it was, he thought, to be willing to engage in such chicanery as that.

It was centuries now since the Piurivars—the Shapeshifters, the Metamorphs, a people with as many names as they had faces—had won full political equality on Majipoor; but, like many young aristocrats of the Mount, Harpirias still harbored some residual prejudices against them. He believed, not entirely incorrectly, that the Shapeshifters were tricky and devious, a race of schemers, slippery and unpredictable, who had never completely reconciled themselves to the occupation of their planet by the billions of humans and other species that had colonized Majipoor nearly fifteen thousand years before. An attempt by the Piurivars hundreds of years ago in the time of Valentine Pontifex to drive all the intruders from their world had failed, as inevitably it had had to, and a detente between the outnumbered Shapeshifters and the dominant humans of Majipoor had been negotiated to everybody's presumable satisfaction. But still—still—

You could never trust them, Harpirias believed. No matter how sincere and helpful they might sound, it was never a good idea to take anything they said at face value, because there was almost always some hidden double meaning, some sly and treacherous subtext to their words. And of *course* Korinaam would see nothing wrong with Harpirias's letting himself pass as Lord Ambinole before the mountaineers. A Shapeshifter—one who by nature was able to assume virtually any physical form he liked—would have no problems with an immoral little masquerade like that.

The caravan moved onward, past the place of the haiguses,

heading out onto the widening plateau. The afternoon now had become bright and clear, and they advanced under a cloudless sky rich with light. Scarcely any vestige remained of the screeching snowstorm through which they had been riding only a few hours before. The air was calm, the sun was high and strong. Scattered dark patches of dampness, speedily vanishing, were the only visible signs of the snowy fury that had whirled down upon them then.

A single huge triangular mountain, like a giant's tooth thrusting upward from the valley, rose directly before them at a great distance, deep purple against the blue of the sky. Stony sharp-contoured hills, covered only by thin and widely spaced stands of graceless scrubby trees and some faint shadowy splashes of bluish grass, bordered their path on both sides as they rode toward it. Now and then Korinaam pointed out animals: the imposing white-furred bulk of a steetmoy standing at the tip of an inaccessible crag; a herd of graceful mazigotivel leaping from one strip of grass to another to graze; a keen-eyed mountain hawk making slow, purposeful circles high overhead.

To Harpirias these Marches seemed to be a place that dwelled perpetually at the edge of some mighty drama. The silence, the immensity of the vistas, the clearness and brightness of the air, the strangeness of the tortured landscape and its few inhabitants—everything intensified the potent impact of the place and kindled high wonder in him. For all his anger at the chain of events that had brought him to these mountains, he could not now regret being here, nor did he doubt he would ever forget the splendor of these sights.

At this time of year the sun remained aloft in these latitudes far into what Harpirias regarded as the normal hours of the night. Since the day did not seem to end, he wondered whether Korinaam would keep them riding onward until midnight or later; but just as hunger was beginning to announce itself to him, the Shapeshifter told him to give the order for a leftward turn into a side canyon opening just before them.

"There's an encampment of March-men in there," Korinaam explained. "They spend their summers in this place. You see the black smoke of the campfire rising, do you? They'll sell us meat for our dinner."

The mountaineers came out to greet them well before the caravan had reached their camp. Evidently they knew Korinaam, and had dealt with him many times before, because they greeted him cordially enough, and there was a long exchange of effusive compliments in a rough, barking kind of mountaineer lingo of which Harpirias could understand only occasional words.

It was Harpirias's first encounter with the nomads of the Marches. He had expected them to be more or less like wild beasts in human form, and indeed they were dressed in roughly sewn hides and not very clean-smelling ones at that, nor did any of them appear to have washed in recent days. At a glance, no one would mistake them for citizens of Ni-moya.

But a close look revealed them to be much less savage than he had imagined. In truth they were robust, vigorous, articulate people with ready smiles and bright alert eyes, who had, actually, very little about them that was primitive or alien. Give them a haircut and a bath and an outfit of clean city clothes and they would pass easily in a crowd. The Skandars, immense hulking four-armed figures covered all over with coarse shaggy fur, were far wilder-looking creatures.

The mountain folk gathered around the travelers in good-natured excitement, offering little trinkets of bone and crude leather sandals for sale. Harpirias bought a few things as mementos of the trip. Some, who spoke more intelligibly than the rest, bombarded him with questions about Ni-moya and other places in Zimroel; and when he told them that in fact he came from Castle Mount, and had lived only a short while in Ni-moya, they grew even more animated, and asked him if it was true that the Coronal's castle had forty thousand rooms, and wanted to know what sort of man Lord Ambinole was, and whether Harpirias himself lived in a grand palace with many servants. Then too they wanted tales of the senior ruler, the Pontifex Taghin Gawad, who was even more mysterious to them, since he never left his imperial seat in the Labyrinth of Alhanroel. Did he really exist, or was he only a figure of myth? If he existed, why had he not picked his own son to be Coronal, instead of the unrelated Ambinole? For what reason were there two monarchs in the world at all, an elder and a younger?

A simple folk, yes. Accustomed to a harsh life, but not unfamiliar with the luxuries of the cities. Most of them had been down into the more civilized parts of Zimroel more than once; a few, apparently, had lived for extended periods in one city or another. They had rejected them, that was all: this was where they preferred to live. But they had not cut themselves off entirely from the great world whose northernmost extremity they happened to inhabit. Simple and unsophisticated they might be, yes, but they were far from savage.

"You'll see real savages soon enough," Korinaam said. "Wait until we reach the country of the Othinor."

5

Harpirias feasted that evening on skewers of grilled meat of a kind unknown to him, and drank mug after mug of a thin, acrid green beer that seemed less intoxicating than it turned out to be. The sun hovered above the rim of the nearby mountains far into the night, and even when it finally dropped from view the sky remained strangely light. He slept in his floater, a fitful and troublesome night's sleep, punctuated by fragmentary dreams and long spells of wakefulness, and awakened with a sour taste in his mouth and an all too predictable throbbing in his head.

In the morning the caravan rolled onward, continuing northward across the plateau. The day was clear and crisp, no sign at all of any new snowstorm. But the terrain grew progressively more bleak hour by hour. With every mile they covered the elevation of the plateau increased moderately but perceptibly, so that Harpirias, looking back, was able to see the road they had traversed, lying far below them.

In this high country the air was chilly even at midday, and there were no more trees here, nor was there much vegetation of any kind, only a few small, practically leafless bushes and isolated scraps of grass. Mainly the landscape consisted of bare rocky hills covered with old gray crusts of ice, over which lay the light dusting of yesterday's storm, barely melted here at all. In the distance, now and then, the fires of other March-men encampments made dark trails of smoke against the sky, but they had no other meetings with any of the mountain folk.

They came at last to the triangular mountain that had stood before them since the last pass: Elminan, it was, the Steadfast Sister. Its true size now became apparent, for at close range it was like an unanswerable wall filling the entire sky with the gigantic question that it posed.

"There is no way over it," said Korinaam. "It can be climbed on this side, but on the other there is no descending. All we can do is go around it."

Which they did: a journey of some days, through rough and ragged country made intractable by long miles of icy ridges hard as iron.

This was a land of wild and hungry beasts that roved with impunity. One morning a pack of ten or twelve shambling great-haunched creatures bigger than Skandars approached the floaters and began energetically to rock them, as if hoping to tip them over and crack them open from below. Harpirias heard one pounding with the force of a giant hammer against the roof of his vehicle. "Khulpoins," Korinaam said. "Very disagreeable."

Harpirias took his energy-thrower from its rack. "I'll try a warning shot, perhaps, to scare them off."

"Useless. Nothing scares them. Give me the weapon."

Reluctantly Harpirias let the Shapeshifter take it from him. Korinaam opened the hatch of the floater a little way and poked the energy-thrower's tube through. Harpirias had a glimpse of wild fiery eyes, slavering jaws, a row of teeth like yellow scythes. Korinaam sighted calmly along the barrel and fired. There was a chilling howl of pain and the khulpoin sprang away from the floater, streams of blood spurting in startling violet gouts from a gaping hole in its shoulder.

"You only wounded it," Harpirias said, with some contempt.

"Exactly. Maximum blood flow, that's the trick. Watch what happens."

The khulpoin, roaring, had begun to run in a lopsided staggering way across the icy ridges, biting frantically at the wound in its shoulder as it went. A trail of purple blood sprang up behind it. Instantly its companions left off their attack on the caravan and gave pursuit. They caught up with it a hundred yards away, surrounding it, clawing at it, leaping upon it as it fell. Even at this distance their growls of satisfaction reverberated through the floater with appalling force.

"Now we leave them to their meal," said Korinaam, sending the floater into high acceleration. Harpirias looked back only once, wincing at what he saw.

A day and a night and a day and a night more, and all the while purple Elminan stood above them like a scornful sentinel; and then at last they reached the mountain's western edge and began to pass around to the far side of it. That transition took another day and a half, until Harpirias found himself looking up at Elminan's north face, a horrifying vertical slab, a sheer straight drop that terminated in a pile of tremendous boulders at ground level. Small wonder there could be no traveling over this mountain, but only around it.

The country beyond was desert-dry and altogether stark. From time to time, as they crossed it, lightning would break without warning or apparent cause out of a cloudless sky, striking the ground with the vehemence of an angry god's wrath and sending up a quick puff of flame. Even Korinaam seemed distressed by this place, and they put it behind them as quickly as they could.

The last of the nine great mountains of the Marches could be seen on the horizon now: two of them lay to the east, Thail and Samaril, the Wise Sister and the Cruel Sister, and to the west, so far away that it was no more than a dark nubbin against the sky, was triple-peaked Kantavinorka, the Eldest Sister. But the route that Korinaam was following took them straight onward, ever northward, past the last campfire of the March-men, past the northernmost zone of known exploration, deep into an empty ice-locked wilderness of perpetual winter, as silent as though it stood under some solemn enchantment. It seemed to Harpirias that they were heading for the roof of the world.

Had anyone ever ventured here before, in all the history of Majipoor? Yes, yes, it must be so: it was clear that Korinaam was familiar with these roads and knew where he was going.

None the less this place seemed to Harpirias like a virgin world, untouched, unknowable. The familiar cities of Majipoor, lying somewhere far behind him in the warm happy haze of summer, had ceased to be real for him: they were dream-cities now, myth-cities, places that had sprouted in the fertile compost of his imagination but could not possibly have any tangible existence. The inconceivably great curve of the giant planet, stretching on and on behind him into the unknown south polar regions, no longer had any substance for him. Only this was real, this bitter land of snow and mist and gleaming rocky walls. Would the journey ever end? No, no, no: he became convinced that he was fated to go on and on forever, deeper and deeper into these bleak and sterile mysteries, led eternally onward by this somber, enigmatic Shapeshifter in a journey to the end of time and space.

But journeys end, even this one.

Korinaam, one morning, gestured toward a dark line that lay against the horizon from east to west, what appeared to be an unbroken vertical wall of stone a hundred times the height of a man that sealed them off from any hope of further advance.

"The domain of the Othinor," he said.

Harpirias looked around, mystified. "Where?"

"Behind that line of mountains."

"But there's no way through!"

"Oh, yes, prince," said Korinaam. "One way. Just one."

It was a wedge-shaped opening in the rock face, a mere crack hardly wider than the floaters themselves. Korinaam needed two days to find it, and there were moments when Harpirias was convinced that the Metamorph had no real idea of where it was; but then, suddenly, the narrow entrance presented itself to them. Korinaam brought the floater to a halt, opened its hatch, signaled to Harpirias to dismount.

"We must enter on foot," the Shapeshifter told him. "It's the only way possible. Come: follow me."

Harpirias disliked leaving the floaters behind; but obviously there was no choice. The vehicles could never fit through this little breach in the rock. Arranging his troops in a double column, the biggest and fiercest-looking Skandars in front, he took his position at the head of the line with Korinaam beside him and marched through into the realm of the Othinor.

He found himself in a secret world of extraordinary beauty and strangeness.

The looming snow-crowned mountain palisade that hid this

place from the awareness of outsiders ran off to the right and left, then curved inward as though to meet and unite with itself, somewhere not too far to the north—thus creating a deep, roughly elliptical pocket canyon, entirely enclosed and shielded by lofty walls of black stone. Within lay a flat shimmering snow field, glinting brilliantly under the noonday sun; and at the farther end of this broad plaza, clustered at the foot of the rock wall, was a shining city made all of ice: sturdy buildings two and even three stories high fashioned from square-hewn blocks of the stuff, laid with impressive precision one atop another and showily bedecked with a bizarre, complex array of fanciful icy parapets and turrets. From their myriad angular surfaces came a thousand thousand dazzling beams of reflected sunlight, like a swarm of diamonds tumbling through the air.

Into this sheltered place the sun would intrude, Harpirias calculated, only for a few hours at a time on just a few days of midsummer. The steep angle at which the canyon wall ascended probably kept the village of the Othinor in shadow all the rest of the year: a claustrophobic place of darkness and mystery, cold and grim. But just now it was radiantly lovely.

As he stood gazing wonderstruck at this eerie little frostbound empire of the high country, figures emerged from the city of ice and began to run across the open plaza toward them.

"The Othinor," Korinaam said. "Remain calm, make no menacing gestures."

They looked like demons. The name "Othinor," Korinaam had explained, meant either "The Hidden Ones" or "The Holy Ones" in the native language: which one was the correct translation was still uncertain. But there was nothing very holy about those who came charging forward now. There were perhaps twenty of them, a band of snarling, hairy, uncouth-looking men, dressed in haphazardly sewn pelts of fur, with jagged stripes of clashing colors painted across their faces and arms. Though they appeared to be armed only with spears and crude swords, they looked ready and eager to go on the offensive against the newcomers.

Harpirias glanced back and saw that some of his Skandars were stirring uneasily. He heard the click of energy-throwers being put in readiness.

"No weapons," he said sharply. "Just stand your ground, and take no action unless we're actually attacked."

It was difficult, even so, to look on nonchalantly as this motley horde of howling devils came rushing toward them. Harpirias threw an uncertain look at Korinaam, who only smiled and said, "They aren't going to harm us. They know who I am and they understand that I've come back with good news for them."

"I hope you're right," muttered Harpirias.

"Hold both your arms outstretched with the palms facing forward: it's a sign of peaceful intentions. Look as dignified and regal as you can and don't say a thing."

Harpirias struck the pose, feeling more than a little foolish. In another moment the Othinor had reached them and surrounded them, capering and dancing in an almost comic show of barbaric force, shouting, sticking out their tongues, waving their swords and spears in their faces with theatrical ardor.

Perhaps that's all it is, thought Harpirias: a show, a staged display of force. Their little way of signifying to strangers that they are not a people to be trifled with.

Korinaam was speaking now: loudly and slowly and clearly, uttering harsh thick-tongued words that had the sound of mere gibberish, though the odd word or two sounded almost familiar. One of the Othinor, a tall gaunt-faced man more elaborately robed and painted than the others, offered a reply, speaking with much greater rapidity; and after a pause Korinaam spoke again, apparently repeating his previous declaration. So it went, for some minutes, one long bewildering stream of palaver after another.

The language of these people, Harpirias began to see, was some distant relative to the language that was spoken everywhere on Majipoor. Like the tongue the March-men spoke, it was a transformed and distorted form of it, scarcely recognizable to a city-dweller. But the divergence had gone even further in this remote northern region. The March-men's speech was actually just a rough-and-ready dialect of standard Majipoori; the strange lingo spoken here, developed during thousands of years of isolation, seemed to have become virtually a different language. How well, Harpirias wondered, did Korinaam understand it?

Well enough, apparently. The Othinor had halted their grotesque capering and were standing quietly in a circle around them. The one who had replied to Korinaam originally—was he the king? No, probably just a priest, Harpirias decided—still was speaking with him, but in a less formal, more conversational way; some of the others, after peering at Harpirias's Skandars and Ghayrogs in unconcealed fascination at the sight of such alien beings, now came up to them to carry out an inspection at closer range.

An Othinor gingerly put his fingertips to the smooth, rigid scales of Mizguun Troyzt, the Ghayrog floater technician, and lightly rubbed them. Though Mizguun Troyzt's cold unblinking eyes remained expressionless, his serpentine hair writhed in emphatic annoyance. He backed away an inch or two, but the Othinor reached out further.

"I do not want to be touched like this," the Ghayrog said to Harpirias, between clenched jaws.

"Nor I," said Eskenazo Marabaud, the captain of the Skandars. An Othinor, standing on tiptoes, had reached up to tug the dense reddish hair that covered the Skandar's great slab of a chest, and now was pulling at the lower of Eskenazo Marabaud's two pairs of arms as though to find out whether they were really attached to his body.

Harpirias fought back laughter. But all the Othinor now

were poking and prodding energetically at the Skandars and Ghayrogs; and he saw that in another moment there was likely to be an incident. "You'd better put a stop to this," he said to Korinaam.

"There is no help for it," the Shapeshifter said. "It is a natural curiosity on their part. Your men will have to get used to it."

"And how long am I supposed to stand with my arms out like this?"

"You can put them down now. We are officially admitted to the village. The priest here tells me that King Toikella is looking forward with much pleasure to making your acquaintance. So come, now, prince: to the royal palace."

6

The palace of the Othinor monarch was, predictably, the grandest of the buildings of the village, a three-storied structure at the extreme eastern end, its flat white facade covered from top to bottom with a scrollwork of fantastic interlaced ice-carvings of the most intricate kind. Within, though, it turned out to be a single cavernous room, enormously high and broad, with no supporting columns. Such construction, thought Harpirias, must surely strain the tensile strength of the ice-blocks out of which the place had been built to its absolute limits.

The great hall was dark and smoky and dank. Its air was stiflingly close, unexpectedly warm, with a foul fishy aroma. Heavy weavings hung from the walls and the floor was strewn with dried rushes that crunched nastily under foot. The only illumination came from a large leather-walled tank, set in a deep pit in the very center of the room, which held a pool of dark oil of some unfamiliar sort that was burning slowly with a bluish flickering glow. Behind it sat King Toikella high atop an astounding platformlike throne made of scores of colossal bones, a whole charnel house of them, tightly and elegantly wedged and woven together—thighbones, ribs, immense curving tusks, shoulderblades, jawbones, an awesome royal seat constructed entirely from the bodies of the formidable beasts that roamed this icy land.

The king himself was well worthy of such a throne: a gigantic potbellied man, entirely bald, strikingly ugly, naked except for a strip of leather around his waist and an array of bone beads and long yellow teeth dangling from a string on his chest. His face and back and shoulders were striped with bright streaks of paint. In his left hand he held a great gross gobbet of bloody, greasy meat, charred on one side but otherwise practically raw, which he had been gnawing on as Harpirias and Korinaam entered. A bevy of half-naked women, most of them as fat and ugly as he was—wives? concubines? royal princesses?—lolled at the foot of the throne.

The Shapeshifter stepped forward, struck what was evidently a ceremonial pose of submission—arms out high, palms turned forward—and greeted the king with a long, slow speech, altogether unintelligible to Harpirias. The king was silent for a time when Korinaam had finished. He tore off a chunk of meat and chewed it reflectively. He looked Harpirias over with care. Then—slowly, solemnly—he rose to his full majestic height, the meat still in his mouth, and spoke for a long while in the deepest voice Harpirias had ever heard come from a human throat. It was a low rumbling growl more like a Skandar's voice than a man's.

When he had finished he pulled another whopping piece of meat from the haunch in his hand and tossed it in an offhand way down to Harpirias, who caught it in some surprise.

"The king bids you welcome," Korinaam murmured.

"Tell him that I thank him for his kindness."

"Not yet. Eat what he's given you, first."

"Are you serious?"

"Extremely. Eat it, prince."

Harpirias stared unhappily at the meat. A sharp, acrid, uninviting aroma rose from it. Only one corner appeared to be cooked at all. The rest of it was bright red, except for the thick vein of fat and gristle that ran through its middle. He turned the hefty chunk over, surreptitiously scanning it for maggots.

"Eat it," the Metamorph said again. "Meat from the king's own portion must not be refused."

"Ah," Harpirias said. "Yes. Yes, certainly."

It was all starting to seem unreal. Civilized, tranquil Majipoor felt very far away. This could well be some strange new universe he had wandered into, or a particularly vivid hallucination. Or perhaps he was asleep, and it was simply a dark sending of the King of Dreams. But if this was a dream he saw no way of waking from it.

Harpirias reminded himself that there were worse things in the world than eating half-raw meat; and also that a diplomat often must make himself conform to the customs of his hosts. He took a bite. The meat wasn't half as bad as it looked. He had tasted less agreeable fare while out hunting in the forests of Castle Mount. The second bite was less pleasing: he had struck the fat, and he had to struggle to keep from gagging. But he recovered and bit into the meat again. King Toikella was watching with interest.

"*Now* thank him for me," Harpirias told the Shapeshifter.

"You haven't finished eating it."

"Neither has he. We can eat while we parley."

"Prince, I think—"

"Give him my thanks," said Harpirias. "This instant."

Korinaam nodded curtly. Turning toward the throne, he launched into a loud, florid-sounding oration. The king listened with apparent pleasure, nodding emphatically after a time and offering a lengthy response of his own, in which, now and again, Harpirias heard the words *Coronal* and *Lord Ambinole* in the midst of the torrent of guttural mountaineer speech. Then Harpirias realized that the king was looking directly at him whenever he pronounced those words.

An ugly suspicion grew in him.

"Wait a minute," he said angrily to Korinaam, when Toikella appeared to have reached the end of his reply. "What have you done? You haven't told him that I'm the Coronal, have you? You know I ordered you not to do that."

The Shapeshifter made an apologetic gesture. "Indeed.

Nor have I done so. But I'm afraid that he himself has jumped to that conclusion, prince."

"Well, unconclude him, then. Now. I'm not going to operate under false pretenses."

Korinaam looked troubled. His form flowed and rippled a little around the edges for a moment, always a sign of acute Shapeshifter distress. "This is not a good time for telling him such a thing. That would only confuse and perhaps anger him, just when everything has begun so smoothly. We'll have plenty of opportunities later to get the matter cleared up."

"*Now,* I said. Not later. He's got to realize that there's been an error, that I'm only the Coronal's emissary, not actually the Coronal. It's an order, Korinaam. I want you to make it absolutely clear to him that—"

But King Toikella had begun speaking again. The Metamorph gestured urgently to Harpirias to be quiet, and Harpirias subsided. In his annoyance he took another bite of his chunk of meat without even noticing.

Harpirias realized glumly that he was completely in the Shapeshifter's power: unable to communicate verbally with King Toikella himself, he was forced to rely on his Metamorph interpreter for every transaction. Korinaam was free to tell the king anything he felt like and Harpirias would never know the truth of what had been said. That could become a problem. Already had, in fact.

Toikella was silent again, waiting.

The Shapeshifter glanced toward Harpirias. "The king declares that he is well pleased you have come," he said.

"Fine. I'd like you to ask him if the hostages are in good health."

"Once again, prince, I must beg your indulgence. The time for asking that is also not just yet."

Another hot jolt of fury shot through Harpirias. "Am I the ambassador, or are you, Korinaam?"

With a sweeping gesture of subservience the Shapeshifter said, "There can be no doubt on that score, prince."

"But nevertheless it seems that you make yourself the final arbiter of what I am allowed to say. In this case I have to insist. Knowing the condition of the hostages is of prime—"

"We must assume that the hostages are in excellent condition, prince," said Korinaam smoothly. "But to ask questions about them at this point would be inappropriate and premature. Worse: it would be impolite."

"Impolite? That naked barbarian sits up there on a throne made out of bones, eating a haunch of practically raw meat and forcing me to do the same, and you tell me that we have to worry about being *polite* to him?"

"Politeness is always useful in these affairs," Korinaam said, giving Harpirias an unctuous smile. "Patience, also. I beg you, prince, to take my advice seriously. I know what these people are like. You do not."

True enough, Harpirias thought.

Nor was it possible in any case to continue the conversation with the king just now, for Toikella had descended from his throne and was bellowing orders to various members of his court in an amazing thunderous voice.

"What's he saying?" Harpirias asked the Metamorph.

"That we are to be shown to our quarters, so that we can have a few hours of rest after our long and arduous journey. There'll be a grand feast tonight in our honor. Othinor hospitality at its finest."

"I can just imagine," said Harpirias unhappily.

By way of guest accommodations the Othinor king provided them with a dozen or so chambers in a low, sprawling icehouse at the opposite end of the village from the royal palace. Harpirias's Skandars had to bunk three or four to a room, cramped though that would be for the bulky creatures; his four Ghayrogs, who liked to keep to themselves, took a pair of rooms; Harpirias and Korinaam each were permitted the luxury of private quarters.

The room they had given Harpirias was a square, boxy windowless cell, lit only by small dim lamps made of carved bone that burned the same thick dark odoriferous oil which had illuminated Toikella's throne chamber. Its air was so still and stagnant, despite the burning lamps, that the enclosure seemed almost to be without air at all; and it was cold—*cold*. Living in it would be like living in a storage refrigerator. Even indoors, his breath rose in steamy clouds before his face.

Everything was ice, the entire structure fashioned of heavy blocks of it—floor and walls and ceiling and all. There was no furniture, only a pile of furry rugs on the floor to serve as a bed.

"Will this be satisfactory, prince?" Korinaam asked him, as he stood frowning in the doorway.

"And if I say no?"

"You will cause the king much embarrassment."

"Certainly I wouldn't want to do that," said Harpirias. "And this is better than sleeping outdoors, I suppose." Though not by very much, he added silently.

"Indeed," replied the Shapeshifter in a solemn tone, and left him to such brief repose as he was able to find in the midst of the stack of thick, itchy furs.

The feast that evening was held in the great high-ceilinged hall that was the royal palace. They had spread heavy rugs, made of white steetmoy hides sewn end to end, over much of the floor—luxurious immaculate rugs that undoubtedly were brought out only on very special occasions. Massive tables of broad rough-hewn planks, resting on substantial trestles fashioned from the same huge bones out of which the royal throne had been constructed, were covered with all manner of plates and tureens and bowls and porringers brimming with foodstuffs. A dozen slender flambeaus projected from sconces of bone set into the walls at the end of arm-shaped handles, providing a smoky, fitful light.

Before the meal there was dancing. The king, seated far above everyone else on the platform that was his throne, rose and clapped his hands, and a dozen musicians playing crude unfamiliar instruments, drums and pipes and gongs and odd-looking stringed devices, set up a discordant screeching polyrhythmic caterwauling at such unthinkable volume that Harpirias feared that the walls of the palace would come crashing down.

The members of the royal harem were the first to dance, a gaggle of tubby bare-breasted women in loincloths and moccasins of black fur, who formed a line and pranced wildly about, kicking up their legs and hurling their arms outward with a berserk manic clumsiness that was both comic and endearing. It was an effort for Harpirias to keep a straight face. But then he realized that the dance was *supposed* to be funny: the dancers themselves were chortling as they cavorted and collided, and whoops of pleasure from the onlookers filled the room, with the king's own mighty roars resounding over all the rest.

Then Toikella himself stepped down from the throne and thrust himself into the line of dancers. He was a formidable figure, half again as tall as any of the women, his shining shaven head rising above them like a mountain dome. His monumental chest was bare, as it had been earlier, but tonight he had donned a cape of black haigus fur that was fastened at his throat to dangle down his back. The haiguses had been stitched together horns and all: angry red eyes gleamed from the pelts, and a triple row of the sharp needles jutted threateningly along the king's heavy-muscled shoulders.

"Eyya!" he boomed. "Halga! Shifta skepta gartha *blin!*"

He moved among the women, stamping his feet, flinging high his arms, bellowing and howling. They swirled around him, no longer comic now but weirdly compelling as they matched his primeval stampings and flingings with fierce, savage steps of their own. It was an awesome sight, ludicrous but frightening at the same time. Harpirias had never seen anything like it.

And now the king seemed to be beckoning to him, bending forward at the waist, staring straight at him, crooking and wriggling his fingers.

Could it be? Were those gestures a summons?

Yes, they were. Harpirias glanced inquiringly toward Korinaam, who nodded. "He's inviting you to dance with him," the Metamorph said. "It's a tremendous honor. It means he regards you almost as an equal."

"Almost an equal. Right."

"You should dance."

"No doubt I should. Yes. Yes, of course I'll dance."

Harpirias hesitated just a moment, studying the steps with closer care, soaking up the strange clashing rhythms. Then he moved out into the center of the floor.

The women slipped back into the shadows. He was alone with the king, who loomed over him like a titan.

Sweat rolled in streams down Toikella's bare glistening body. He grinned in high amusement—Harpirias noticed for the first time that there were bright gems, an emerald and a ruby and a third one of a darker hue, set into his front teeth—and struck his hands together three times. It was a signal, apparently, to the musicians, who halted their frenzied wailing and honking and pounding and screeching and set about playing a different tune entirely, one that was slow and sinuous, a dark, quiet, serpentine melody, haunting and strange.

The king, his shoulders hunched high and his hands held facing each other with fingers writhing mysteriously, began now to move with implausible grace in a wide circle around Harpirias, treading lightly, almost floating. It could have been the dance of a hunter stalking his prey.

Harpirias, having no idea of what step he was meant to undertake, remained still for a moment, watching Toikella in the baffled fashion of one who is beginning to slip into a trance. But then he too started to move, almost without conscious volition: flexing his fingers first, then slowly raising and lowering his shoulders, and finally mimicking the king's fastidious tiptoe delicacy as he set out to follow his own circular path, going in the direction opposite to Toikella's.

For long moments they stalked each other, winding round and round, the immense fleshy man and the shorter, more compact one, while the music gradually grew and grew in tempo and volume. Soon it began to approach the wild intensity of the women's dance. Harpirias picked up his pace as the music rose. Toikella, still grinning, moved faster as well. Harpirias laughed. It was impossible now to maintain his earlier delicacy of step. He leaped; he bounded; he stamped his feet and clapped his hands.

"Eyya!" cried the king. "Halga!"

"Eyya!" Harpirias echoed. "Halga!"

"Shifta skepta gartha *blin!*"

"Shifta skepta!"

"Gartha blin!"

"Shifta skepta gartha *blin!*"

Harpirias threw his head back, flung his hands high, pulled one knee almost to his chest and then the other. He howled and roared. He stamped and clapped. And he saw now that others were coming out onto the floor, some of the women first, and then the elaborately robed man with the painted face who had spoken with Korinaam at the entrance to the valley, and other men after him, flamboyantly painted also—high warriors of the tribe, perhaps. Even a few of the Skandars joined the dance, finally, although none of the Ghayrogs did, nor did Korinaam venture forth. For what seemed like hours they all circled round the room like a band of moonstruck madmen, until abruptly the music died away in mid-note, as if all the musicians had perished in the same instant, and the only sounds in the room were those of laughter and harsh breathing.

The king, who was standing beside Harpirias as the music

ended, turned toward him. There was a look of total delight in the big man's eyes. He reached out one outsized paw for him and gathered Harpirias in, drawing him into a crushing embrace. For a seemingly endless moment the king held him there. The royal effluvium was overwhelming: a reeking mixture of sweat, animal grease, thickly applied pigments, awful perfumes.

Then Toikella released him, grinned once more, and clapped his forehead in what had the look of a salute. Harpirias, grinning also, returned the gesture. The dance had left him exhilarated. He felt almost like himself again, after all these long gloomy months of exile. To his surprise, he found himself oddly charmed, too, by Toikella, who seemed to be an amiable, high-spirited old tyrant. It appeared that Toikella was taken by him as well.

Yes, Harpirias thought, we will be the best of friends, he and I. We will sit up late together and drink whatever it is that they like to drink in this place, and we will tell each other the stories of our lives. Friends, yes. Bosom companions.

It was time for the feasting, finally.

The king served Harpirias with his own hands: a high honor, evidently, but something of a doubtful one, since diplomatic courtesy now obliged Harpirias to eat everything that Toikella had chosen for him. Left to his own discretion, he might have preferred a less generous assortment, for nearly everything on the serving tables looked and smelled inedible.

Most of it was meat, roasts and stews and skewered strips, buried under thick, pungent sauces. There were several soups—Harpirias hoped that those fluids were soups, and nothing more sinister—and mounds of roasted nuts, and vegetable mushes of various kinds, and what might have been gnarled roots, baked until charred. The beverage of choice evidently was some kind of bitter, brackish beer, grayish-black in color, that bubbled unpleasantly of its own accord in the bowl.

Harpirias ate what he could, nibbling here, staunchly cramming there, washing it all down with desperate gulps of the beer. These people seemed to like their meat half-cooked and fatty, and most of it had a gaminess which even an experienced huntsman like Harpirias found hard to tolerate. All the sauces were much too spicy for him, and many of the vegetable dishes had a spoiled or fermented undertaste. But he did his best. He understood what a sacrifice it must be for the Othinor to provide such abundance as this, living as they did in a land that was covered by snow most of the year, where farming was unknown, where every scrap of food must be pried from nature's unwilling grasp.

The king plied him with second portions, and thirds, and fourths. Harpirias laughed and protested, and confined his eating to nibbles, and let the royal servants clear his unfinished plates away whenever Toikella was looking the other way.

The evening wore on. And on and on.

Three clowns entered the room and carried out a long unfathomable routine of jokes and haphazard juggling that brought tears of mirth to the king's face. The women danced again, and then a group of the men. Harpirias grew drowsy, but gamely compelled himself to pay attention. He drank more of the bubbling bitter beer: it was almost possible to like it, after a while. Gradually he became aware that the feasters were beginning to slip away, in groups of two and three. The big room had grown very quiet. The king had gathered two armloads of his women to his side and had slumped down with them onto the rugs.

Softly Korinaam said, "Come, prince. The evening is at its end."

"Shall I bid the king good night?"

"He won't notice, I suspect." Indeed, Toikella appeared preoccupied. Soft moist slobbering sounds could be heard. "We should just go," the Shapeshifter said.

Together they crossed the icy plaza to the guest house at the far end. It was late enough so that darkness had fallen. The air on this midsummer night was clear and crisp, and had what Harpirias regarded as a wintry edge to it. The stars hardly seemed to shimmer: they were discrete points of light, keenly bright.

"You did well tonight," said Korinaam, as they entered the building of ice. "A good start to the mission."

Harpirias nodded. He felt woozy. Too much stimulation, too much strange beer, too much bad food, too much close smoky air. He pushed the leather door-flap aside and went into his room. It was even warmer inside than the throne room had been, and the lamps, which had been lit during his absence, had filled the air with thick oily smoke, so that Harpirias choked and gagged at the first breath of it.

There was someone in the room. A woman.

"Yes?" he said. "What do you want?"

She rose and came toward him, displaying a gap-toothed smile. Harpirias recognized her as one of those who had clustered earlier at the foot of King Toikella's throne—the youngest-looking and least unattractive of them, in fact, a reasonably slender girl with straight, glossy dark hair cut in a bowl shape just about to the level of her ears. She was wearing only the moccasins and loincloth of black fur that had been the costume of the dancers, and now, quite casually, she pulled the loincloth down and kicked it aside. With a cheerful gesture she pointed toward the pile of sleeping-furs, tapped her chest, extended her hand to him.

"No," Harpirias said. "Not tonight, thanks. I'm very, very tired. I'd just like to go to sleep."

She bobbed her head up and down and giggled. She pointed again to the furs.

Harpirias stayed where he was. "You didn't understand a word of what I said, did you? No. No, how could you?"

For an instant he was almost tempted. He had been living chastely for so long now that chastity was starting to feel almost like a normal way of life to him, which was a situation that surely needed to be remedied. But not here, not now, not with her. She was far from hideous—pleasing features, alert mischievous eyes, a decent figure, appealing breasts—but she was, after all, barbaric in her manner and dirty and unfragrant in her person. And he *was* extremely tired and not at all interested.

It was flattering that she had taken a fancy to him, he supposed. But what would the king say when he discovered that the ambassador from the civilized world had allowed himself a night's sport with a member of the royal harem?

"I'm sorry," he said gently. "Perhaps another time." He picked up her discarded loincloth and pressed it into her hand. Then, putting the tips of his fingers lightly and he hoped unprovocatively against her back, he steered her toward the door, not exactly pushing her but making it as clear as he could that he was asking her to go.

She turned and looked back at him for a long charged moment. Sadly? Angrily? Mockingly? He couldn't tell.

Then she was gone.

Shaking his head, Harpirias did what he could to cleanse himself and get ready for sleep. He was on the verge of climbing between two of the furs on the floor when the Shapeshifter's quiet voice from the hallway said, "May I speak with you, prince?"

Harpirias yawned. This was getting very annoying. He

said, without rising to pull back the sheet of leather that functioned as the door, "What is it, Korinaam?"

"The girl you refused has come to me."

"My warmest congratulations. I wish you much joy of her."

"You misunderstand me, prince. She came to me to ask what she has done wrong with you, why she has displeased you. She has gone away bewildered and insulted."

"She has? Well, that's too bad, I suppose. It wasn't my intention to hurt her feelings. But I didn't particularly want company tonight, not hers, not anybody's. And as a general rule it doesn't seem smart to me to be sleeping with the king's wives."

"Not one of his wives, prince. It is King Toikella's youngest daughter whom you have rejected. And when he learns of it, there's bound to be no small amount of trouble."

"His *daughter?* He wants me to go to bed with his daughter?"

"It is traditional Othinor courtesy," said the Shapeshifter. "You really must not refuse."

Appalled, Harpirias pressed both his hands to his forehead. Was Korinaam serious? Yes, yes, he must be. For a wild moment Harpirias debated asking the Metamorph to summon the girl back; but then a mounting sense of vexation overcame the force of whatever presumable obligations of diplomacy he might be under. He wanted to get some sleep. There were limits to the things he was supposed to do for the sake of getting this treaty signed. He was *not* going to sleep with a smelly savage girl simply to keep King Toikella happy. Not. Not. Not. Not.

Thinking quickly, Harpirias said, "You will tell the king, when and if the matter comes up, that I am highly appreciative of the honor he has paid me. But in fact I have taken a severe vow of abstinence from physical pleasure as one of the disciplines of my high office. Under its terms I mustn't allow myself to be approached by a woman."

"You have said nothing of this before, prince."

"I'm saying it now. A vow of abstinence. Is that understood?"

"It is, yes."

"Thank you. Good night, Korinaam."

He pulled one of the furs over his head, skin side out. It smelled as though they had tanned it in steetmoy urine.

This was all going to be even more difficult than he had expected, he told himself. If his dear friend Tembidat and his beloved cousin Vildimuir had happened to be within his reach just now, he would with a good deal of pleasure have wrung their necks.

7

The next day passed slowly and strangely. Hardly anyone was awake and about in the village when Harpirias went outside in the morning: only some nearly naked children, playing games of pursuit along the base of the high rocky wall that enclosed the settlement, and half a dozen women of the tribe laying out strips of freshly butchered meat to dry in the one narrow strip of sunlight that was able to penetrate the canyon. The meat was meant to be put away, he assumed, against the winter that would all too soon arrive.

Gradually the place came to life. The day was warm, the sky was bright and clear. A party of hunters assembled down near the palace and solemnly filed off toward the nearby cliffs. Some old women carried a stack of hides into the sunny part of the plaza and squatted in a circle to scrape them with bone knives. A limping musician came out of a house, knelt cross-legged on the ice, and played a single thin tune on a bone pipe for more than an hour, over and over.

At noon the gaunt-faced high priest—for so Harpirias had come to regard him—emerged from the royal palace and strode to a large flat slab of black stone, no doubt an altar of some sort, that rose a few inches above the icy floor of the plaza in the open space midway between the canyon entrance and the clustered buildings of the village. He was bearing a crudely painted clay jug, from which, once he had reached the altar, he drew seeds or nuts of some sort that he hurled toward the four corners of the world. An offering to the gods, Harpirias supposed.

Of the king and the other members of his court there was no sign all morning. "He is a late sleeper," Korinaam said.

"I envy him, then," Harpirias said. "I was awake at dawn, half sweltering and half freezing. When will the negotiating sessions begin, do you think?"

"Tomorrow, perhaps. Or the day after. Or the day after that."

"No sooner?"

"The king is never in any hurry."

"But I am," said Harpirias. "I want to be out of here before the next winter begins."

"Yes," the Metamorph replied. "I don't doubt that you do."

Something about the way he said that was not very encouraging.

Harpirias thought of the eight paleontologists—or perhaps there were ten; no one seemed quite sure—who at this moment were held prisoner somewhere not far from here. *They* knew what winter was like in Othinor country. They had spent a year living somewhere near here in dark frigid cages, probably, eating mush and acrid gruel, scraps of cold fatty meat, bitter roots, nuts. Very likely they were more than a little weary of this place by now. But the king was never in any hurry, said Korinaam. And Korinaam should know.

Harpirias tried to accommodate himself to the slow rhythms of the place. The life of the village, he had to admit, was fascinating in its way. Surely this was how primitive people had lived thousands of years ago, hundreds of thousands, really, in that almost mythical era when Old Earth had been the one and only home of mankind and the idea that human beings might journey to the stars was the wildest kind of fantasy. The daily routine, the hunting and gathering of food, the preparing and storing of it, the endless making of simple tools and weapons, the rituals and observances and little superstitious customs, the children's games, the sudden inexplicable eruptions of laughter or singing or loud dispute that subsided just as suddenly—it all made Harpirias feel as though he had slipped backward in time to some distant epoch of mankind's primeval past. He would very much rather have been among his friends on Castle Mount just now, drinking the rich potent wine of Muldemar and swapping lively tales of intrigue and chicanery among the dukes and princes of the Coronal's entourage; but he had to admit that what he was experiencing here was something that was granted to very few, and which he might actually look back upon fondly and gratefully, some day far in the future.

The king came out of his palace, finally, late in the afternoon. Harpirias, who was playing a game of knucklebone in the plaza with Eskenazo Marabaud and a couple of the other Skandars, watched with amazement as the king paused, turned, peered blankly at them a moment with no sign of recognition or interest on his face, and moved along his way.

"As if he didn't even notice us," Harpirias murmured.

"Maybe he didn't," said Eskenazo Marabaud. "Kings see only what they want to see. Perhaps he doesn't feel like seeing us today."

A shrewd observation, Harpirias thought. Yesterday Toikella had been all solicitude and generosity; today he took no more notice of the ambassador and his troops than he would have of a visiting party of fleas. Was this the king's way of letting the visitors from the outer world know that events unfolded only on Toikella time in the land of the Othinor?

Or—and this was a more troublesome possibility—had he taken offense at Harpirias's crass and blunt rejection of his daughter's favors?

Whatever the reason, there were no negotiations that day, nor any contact with the king whatsoever. The members of the embassy were left to amuse themselves all afternoon. No one spoke with them or even paid any particular attention to them as they wandered through the village.

Toward evening three Othinor women brought the visitors their dinner aboard heavy sleds that they dragged with evident effort across the plaza: a side of cold meat, a tub of the gray-black beer that had gone flat, a tangled mound of roasted roots, all of it obviously leftovers from last night's feast. It was meager fare.

"I think there may be some trouble here," Harpirias said to Korinaam.

"Try to be more patient, prince. All this is normal. The king is establishing his control over us."

"But we can't *let* him have control over us!"

"That doesn't mean he won't make the attempt. He is a king, after all."

"A barbarian king."

"A king all the same. In his own eyes he is the equal of the Coronal and the Pontifex together. You should never forget that, prince. He will speak with us in his own good time. This is only the first day."

"A day of idleness makes me restless."

"Which is what he wants to achieve," said Korinaam. "Thus he puts you at a disadvantage. Patience, prince. Patience."

There was another strangeness after dinner, a considerable

one. As Harpirias stepped out of the guest house for some fresh air, just when dusk was falling, he caught sight of a flare of brightness along the rim of the canyon wall, indeed at its highest point, far up over the side of the village where the royal palace was. It was as though someone had lit a beacon fire up there.

Perhaps this was something they did every night here, he thought. Sending some agile boy of the tribe to the top of the wall to ignite the torch of evening. But no, no, this had the appearance of an unusual event, for the plaza now was filling with tribesfolk, pointing, chattering. A girl ran into the palace to summon Toikella, and he came out in swift strides, all but naked in the evening chill, craning his neck and shading his eyes against the brightening moonlight as he stared upward.

Harpirias centered all his concentration on the place where he had seen that bright flare; and shortly it became clear to him that there were tiny dark figures up there, no bigger than insects at this distance, just next to the bonfire on the canyon rim. They appeared to be struggling with something that they were trying to push over the edge of the canyon, a big black bundle of some sort, very bulky and difficult to maneuver. After another few moments they succeeded: Harpirias watched it fall, rebounding off the side of the canyon two or three times as it plunged, striking a horn-shaped rocky knoll and catching there briefly, then coming free and plummeting straight to the canyon floor to land with a monstrous thudding sound practically in front of the palace.

The body of a huge animal, it was: a thick-legged coarse-furred thing with great crescent tusks, a giant grazing beast, perhaps, a descendant of the formidable mountain-dwelling creature which according to Metamorph myth had brought the primordial inhabitants of Majipoor into being by licking them out of an icy cliff.

It lay now on the ice of the plaza in a somber motionless heap—a vast shaggy black mound from which bright streams of blood were flowing. The king, muttering and frowning, walked around it and around again, prodding and tugging at it. Plainly he was deeply disturbed. Harpirias realized that the animal must have been deliberately mutilated before it was thrown over the cliff; not only had its throat been slashed but red slashes showed through the heavy fur along its flanks and belly where deep cuts had been made in geometrical patterns.

What must have been nearly the entire population of the village had assembled by now to inspect this phenomenon that had dropped from on high. The tiny figures were no longer visible along the rim of the canyon, and the bonfire, though still smoldering, was almost out.

Harpirias looked toward Korinaam. "Do you understand what any of this means?"

The Shapeshifter shook his head. "A mystery to me, prince. When I was here last year I never saw anything like it."

"Neither have they, apparently." Harpirias nodded toward Toikella, who was huddling with the high priest and a few of the other courtiers in a circle around the fallen animal. "Go over to them. See what you can find out."

But Korinaam had no success in gaining the attention of Toikella and his men. They seemed not even to hear him when he spoke to them. After a while he turned away and conferred briefly with one of the lesser tribesmen and then another before coming back to Harpirias.

"The animal," reported the Shapeshifter, "is called a hajbarak. It's looked upon as a sacred beast. There's a small herd of them that roams the mountains just back of here, and only the king is permitted to hunt them. For anyone else to kill one is an act of major sacrilege. The biggest of the bones from which his throne is made are hajbarak bones."

"What is this, then, a declaration of war from some hostile tribe?"

"So far as I know, no other tribes live in this region, hostile or otherwise."

"So far as you or anyone knew, the Othinor didn't live here either, until somebody discovered them. Obviously there's somebody else up there."

"Obviously," said Korinaam, with some testiness in his tone. "But whether the ones who threw the animal down here are from an enemy tribe, or are simply outcasts from this one, I have no idea. The first man I spoke to was so shocked that he didn't seem capable of talking to me at all. The second one told me only that the animal was sacred and that this should not have happened. You are free to draw your own conclusions, prince."

But he had none to draw; nor was the Shapeshifter able to learn anything from the villagers the next day. They simply would not speak of what had happened.

The chief consequence of the evening's strange event, so far as Harpirias was concerned, was that it produced an additional postponement of the opening of negotiations. The king was closeted in the palace all that day, and the next. The dead animal had been dragged away to the accompaniment of solemn choral chanting; the place where it had struck the ground had been cleansed of all blood; sentries were posted day and night in the plaza to watch the canyon rim for signs of new intrusion.

Then came a messenger to Harpirias in the morning with word that the king was ready at last to confer with him.

"You will tell him, as the very first topic of discussion, that I am not the Coronal Lord Ambinole," Harpirias said to the Metamorph as they crossed the plaza toward the palace.

"Not the very first thing, prince. Please."

"One of the first, then."

"Let me be the judge of the proper timing for this."

"The proper timing," Harpirias said, "was the very moment that the confusion began."

"Yes, perhaps that is so. But it was inappropriate to interrupt the king then to make the correction. And now—"

"I want this thing cleared up, Korinaam."

"Of course. As soon as it's feasible."

"And from this moment on," Harpirias said, "whenever I address a remark of any sort to the king, I want you to translate it literally and exactly. Likewise I want an exact and literal translation of whatever the king may say to me."

"Certainly, prince. Certainly."

"You know, I'm actually not as stupid as you may think, and it's not beyond my powers to start learning this language that they speak here myself. If I should discover that you haven't been a totally honest interpreter, Korinaam, I'll kill you."

The blunt word so startled Korinaam that he was galvanized into an involuntary moment of metamorphosis. The contours of his body blurred and fluttered, his fragile elongated form thickening and drawing into itself as if for protection; his color deepened from pale green to a dark shade of teal; his face sealed itself so that his eyes and lips could barely be seen. With a gasp and a shiver of his shoulders he recovered his normal semblance and said:

"*Kill,* prince?"

"Kill. The way I would kill an animal in the forest."

"I have not deceived you in any way," said the Shapeshifter. "Nor do I intend to do so hereafter."

"Better not even to think of it," Harpirias said.

He was surprised to find King Toikella in a jovial, even exuberant mood. The curious happening of a few nights before did not appear to be casting its shadow on him today. Nor was there any trace of the remoteness, the coldness, that he had displayed the one time he and Harpirias had encountered each other since the evening of the feast.

Toikella was down from his throne, energetically pacing around the great hall. As usual he was surrounded by his women—Harpirias noted uneasily the presence of the young princess who had come to his room to offer herself to him—and the king would pause from time to time in his restless perambulation to give this one a rough caress, to mutter something hoarse and perhaps affectionate into the ear of that one. When he saw Harpirias entering he whirled and called out a loud raucous salutation in which Harpirias detected the Othinor word *helminthak*—which from its context Harpirias had already come to think meant "majesty," "lordship," some such title of honor—and the words *Coronal* and *Lord Ambinole* once again.

Harpirias glowered at Korinaam. This error was becoming perpetuated and ever more difficult to eradicate.

But there was no chance now to do anything about it. The king, amidst deafening gusts of laughter, had thrown his arm about Harpirias and was bellowing a lengthy string of incomprehensible exclamations into his ear. After a time Harpirias extricated himself more or less tactfully from the big man's smothering embrace and looked toward the Shapeshifter.

"What did he say?"

"He was welcoming you back to his court."

"There was more to it than that. There had to be."

Korinaam's shape wavered just a little at the edges.

"I want an exact translation," Harpirias told him. "Or else." He drew one finger swiftly across his Adam's apple.

"What the king was saying," the Shapeshifter replied, rolling his eyes, "is that he wonders what kind of race the Majipoori can be, if they are ruled by such an effeminate king."

"What?"

"You asked for an exact translation, prince."

"Yes. I know that. But what does he mean, 'effeminate'? He's talking about me, isn't he, and not the real Lord Ambinole? What possible reason could he have for believing—"

"I think," said the Metamorph cautiously, "that he is referring to your rejection of his daughter on the night of the feast."

"Ah. Ah. Of course. Tell him—tell him, first, that I am not the king of Majipoor, but simply the king's ambassador. Thank him, then, for his kindness in sending his beautiful daughter to visit me the other night. And then let him know that I am not in any way effeminate, as he will see if he cares to take me hunting with him in the royal game preserves. But tell him also about the vow of chastity that I have taken, which separates me for a time from the embrace of women for the benefit of my soul."

Korinaam spoke briefly to the king—too briefly, Harpirias thought, considering all that he had asked him to say. Toikella laughed again, even more vociferously than before, and made a quick, blunt-sounding answer.

"Well?" Harpirias asked.

"The king says that he thinks you would do well to get yourself released from such a stupid and injurious vow."

"I can see where he would take that position. But at the present time I intend to continue living a life of bodily purity. Tell him that."

Korinaam spoke again. So did the king, for quite some time.

"He admires your determination, prince. But he says that a vow of chastity seems as strange to him as snow that falls upwards. He himself has eleven wives and makes love to at least three of them every night. More than a hundred of the citizens of the village are his children."

"My congratulations to him on his energy, and on his fertility also." Harpirias narrowed his gaze. "And how did he react when you told him I wasn't the Coronal?"

More wavering at the edges. "I did not tell him that, prince."

"I recall instructing you to translate everything I say exactly, upon pain of death, Korinaam."

"Yes. Quite. I understand completely, prince. But how can I make you see that this is not something that I can simply drop into a conversation about other things? The king expected the Coronal to come in person. He believes that you are he. Telling him the contrary now could well wreck everything before it has even begun."

"Korinaam—!"

The Metamorph held up his hand. "Once again I beg you, prince, allow me to choose the proper time for setting this matter straight, and give me no more orders concerning the subject for now. Or threats," Korinaam added after a pause.

Harpirias closed his eyes a moment. It was essential to gain some control over these interchanges, or he was lost.

"Tell the king," Harpirias said sternly, even though Toikella was in the midst of speaking again, "that I would now like to discuss with him the issue of the hostages. In particular I request permission to visit them without further delay so that I can satisfy myself that they are in good condition."

"My good prince—"

"Tell him."

"I beg you—"

Harpirias made the finger-across-throat gesture again.

Korinaam gave him a sour look. Then he turned toward King Toikella and began once more to speak.

8

The discussion went on for quite some time. Harpirias strained his ears, desperately trying to pick out key words to remember and have translated for him afterward. The Shapeshifter was entirely too slippery; he must try to learn a little of the Othinor tongue himself.

A new word had entered the parley, at any rate—*goszmar,* is what it sounded like. Harpirias heard it over and over again. He hoped that it was the Othinor word for "hostages," that for once Korinaam had actually obeyed him in regard to the topic of conversation. *Goszmar, goszmar, goszmar*—it was bandied back and forth for what seemed to be an hour. Finally the Shapeshifter turned to Harpirias and said, "It wasn't easy. As I've told you, he hates to be hurried. But he has agreed to let you see them this very afternoon, when his men bring them their regular meal."

"Fine. Where are they?"

"An ice-cave on the side of the mountain, high above the

north end of the valley. He says the climb is extremely strenuous and difficult."

"Especially for an effeminate lordling like me, I suppose. Let him know that I look forward enthusiastically to the chance for a little exercise."

"I already have, prince."

"Have you, now? How very thoughtful of you, Korinaam."

As it turned out, "strenuous" was a moderate term indeed for the ascent of the mountain. Young as he was, strong as he was, Harpirias found himself pushed almost to the edge of his endurance. The route, narrow and rough, went by way of a maddening series of hairpin switchbacks that traced a slowly rising curve along the face of the canyon wall. Menacing jagged rocks, half-hidden in the snow-speckled trail, jutted upward from it every few yards, offering the unwary climber the possibility of tripping and slipping and plunging into the ever-deepening chasm that yawned without a guard rail at their left elbows. The air grew colder and colder as they rose, and powerful gusts of icy wind beat remorselessly at their faces. Ungainly big-beaked birds, roused from their nests amongst the crags, flapped screeching about their heads, beating at the intruders with broad powerful wings.

These were unaccustomed privations. The muscles of Harpirias's legs quickly began to protest. Bands of pain sprang up across his breast and gut. His eyes ached, his nostrils stung. But he made a point of concealing even the slightest indication that he found the climb a struggle. This was a test which he had insisted upon taking, and he knew he must pass it.

With him he had brought not only Korinaam but also the Skandar Eskenazo Marabaud, whose size and strength would make him a comforting presence. Five of the Othinor accompanied them: the high priest and four men of the warrior caste. The king stayed behind, having excused himself from the climb with a show of such cool insouciant self-regard that Harpirias could only be charmed by the man's audacity. "I would go with you in a minute, and gladly so," Toikella explained. "But my people need me always close at hand. I must never ignore their wishes." Was that a wink? Harpirias wondered. And a royal smirk?

The path took them over crackling crusts of hardened snow and then across a perilous-looking bridge of ice. Below that flimsy span passed a rushing stream that came spurting from the heart of the cliff like a gush of dark blood. Beyond it the switchbacks abruptly ended and the trail shot straight upward at a heart-straining angle over loose gravelly rocks glazed by ice. Harpirias's bare fingertips turned numb and he thought his chest would crack from the coldness of the air.

And this was summer! Othinor summer! By the Lady, how did these people survive the winters in this place? Were they made of stone? Did icy waters flow in their veins?

The air up here was thin and pale. Harpirias told himself that he could see right through it, and then asked himself in some perplexity what he had meant by that. Was his mind beginning to give way under the stress of the climb? He warned himself to be on guard against nonsensical thoughts. The altitude, the latitude—the attitude, he added—*the altitude, the latitude, the attitude*—the words ran through his mind over and over, an infuriatingly relentless jingle.

The others evidently were having no trouble with the climb. All the Othinor but the priest were carrying heavy sacks of provisions for the prisoners, without the slightest difficulty. Eskenazo Marabaud actually appeared to be enjoying himself more and more as the difficulties of the ascent increased. Even the flimsily built Korinaam was striding readily along. Harpirias found that mortifying; but he reminded himself that his companions all were people of cold-weather climates, accustomed to such harsh conditions as these. He, young and strong as he was, had lived all his life in the gentle climes of Castle Mount.

He looked down once, only once. The village was a mere outline, white against white, a collection of distant tiny boxes huddling against the mountain wall. The sight dizzied him and he swayed, but Eskenazo Marabaud reached out easily with his lower left hand to steady him.

They were not far below the rim of the wall now. Harpirias could see it, a wide flat summit, stretching back away from him. Here the trail turned a corner and unexpectedly broadened to two or three times its usual width. A short way below the summit a dark uneven oval in the face of the cliff announced the presence of a cave. Boulders were piled high to block its mouth; two fur-clad Othinor armed with swords stood guard before it, their arms folded, their faces expressionless.

The high priest—Mankhelm was his name—said a few brusque words to them. The sentinels saluted and made haste to roll back the uppermost level of the boulders so that they could enter.

All was dark within. There was a long business of lighting torches; and then Harpirias saw that they were in a low-roofed cavern, deep and narrow, that ran back far into the core of the rocky wall. Seepage from some mountain spring had coated its sides everywhere with an icy skin, which glinted with a beautiful bluish sheen by the torches' smoky glow.

Shadowy figures came lurching out of the cavern's depths, blinking and murmuring as they approached the light.

In a formal tone Harpirias said, "I am the ambassador of His Highness Lord Ambinole, come to win your freedom for you. Harpirias is my name. Prince Harpirias of Muldemar."

"Divine be praised! What year is this?"

"What—year?" Harpirias was taken aback. "Why, the thirteenth of the Pontificate of Taghin Gawad. Does it seem that you've been here so long?"

"Forever. Forever."

Harpirias stared. The man with whom he spoke was tall and terribly thin, pale as bleached parchment, with a crest of wiry graying hair fanning far out in every direction from his balding scalp and a thick, unkempt black beard covering nearly all of his face. Two burning half-crazed eyes peered from that thicket of hairy growth. He was dressed in loose fraying rags, pitifully inadequate to the cold.

"You've been here only a year," Harpirias told him. "Or perhaps just a little more. It's the middle of the summer in the Marches. The summer of the year Thirteen."

"Only a year," the man repeated in wonder. "It feels like a lifetime. —I am Salvinor Hesz," he announced, after a moment. Harpirias knew the name. The leader of the ill-starred paleontological expedition, yes.

Others much like him in their raggedness and gauntness stood gathered behind. Harpirias counted quickly: six, seven, eight, nine. Nine. Was one missing?

"Is this the entire group of you?" he asked.

"All of us, yes."

"There was some question about how many of you had made the journey. Eight, ten—the records were unclear."

"Nine," said Salvinor Hesz. "Changes of personnel were made at the last minute. Two dropped out—what luck for them!—and one replacement was found."

"Myself," a man of remarkable height and thinness said, in a black sepulchral voice that seemed to rise from the bottom of the Great Sea. "It was my good fortune to be allowed to join the expedition just as it was leaving Ni-moya. What an opportunity for furthering my career!" He put out a trembling hand. "My name is Vinin Salal. How much longer are we to be kept here?"

"I've only just arrived," said Harpirias. "There's a formal treaty to negotiate with the king before you can be freed. But I hope to have you out of here before the summer ends. I *will* have you out of here by then." He looked from one to another of them, marveling at the fleshlessness of them all. Skin and bones was all they were. "By the Lady, they've been starving you, haven't they? They'll pay for this! Tell me: what kind of treatment have you had?"

"They feed us twice a day," Salvinor Hesz said, without rancor. He gestured to the sacks of provisions which the Othinor had thrown down against the side of the cave, and which the men of the cavern appeared to be in no hurry to fall upon. "Dried meat, nuts, roots—pretty much the same things they eat themselves. It isn't a diet one can love. But they do feed us."

"Every morning, every afternoon, very punctually. A party of them always comes climbing up here with these sacks of food for us," one of the others said. "Sometimes we can hear terrible storms raging outside, but they never miss a meal, they come up here all the same. You don't get plump on Othinor fare, you know. Still, we can hardly say that we're being starved."

"No," someone else agreed. "Not starved, no."

"No."

"Not at all."

"Treated quite well, in fact."

"Decent people. Very backward but not unkind, all things considered."

Harpirias was puzzled by the mildness of their words, the almost benign tone in which they spoke of their savage captors. These men looked like walking skeletons. They had lived a year and something more in this dark glacial hole, far from their homes and loved ones and careers, slowly wasting away on the odds and ends of repellent food that was all the Othinor could provide. Where was their fury? Why were they not raining down curses on their jailers? Had this imprisonment so broken their souls that they were grateful even for the miserable bits and pieces that those who had condemned them to lie here were giving them to eat?

He had heard that prisoners, after many a month and year, sometimes came to love their keepers. But that was a hard thing for him to understand.

"You have no grievances against the Othinor at all?" Harpirias asked. "Other than having been forced to remain here against your will, I mean?"

They met his question with silence. It seemed to be difficult for these men to think clearly. Their minds as well as their bodies must have been weakened by their privations, Harpirias thought. The hunger, the cold, the separation from the world.

Then Salvinor Hesz said, "Well, they've taken our specimens away. The fossils. That was very distressing. You must try to get them back for us."

"The fossils," said Harpirias. "So you did actually find the bones of these land-dragons?"

"Oh, yes, yes. Quite a spectacular find. A clear link to the maritime species of dragons—an unquestionable evolutionary connection."

"Is it, now?"

"We succeeded in excavating teeth of astonishing size, ribs, vertebrae, fragments of a huge spinal column—" Salvinor Hesz's lean face became radiant with excitement. He glowed through the bushy shroud of his beard. "The largest land creatures that ever existed on this world, by far. And beyond any real doubt the ancestors of our sea-dragons—perhaps a transitional evolutionary form, one that will need a great deal of further study. The bones of their ears indicate clearly that they were designed to hear both on land and under water, for example. We've uncovered an entire new chapter in our knowledge of the development of life on Majipoor. And there's more, much more, waiting to be discovered on that hillside. We had only just finished our scaffolding and begun to dig when the Othinor found us and took us prisoner."

"And confiscated everything we had uncovered," said another. "Reburied it, so we were given to understand."

"That's the most maddening part of all," came a voice from farther back in the cavern. "Having made a major discovery like that, and not being able to bring our findings back to civilization. We can't leave here without those things. You *will* insist on the return of the fossils, won't you?"

"I'll see what I can do, yes."

"And also to get their permission to continue the work. You need to make them see that our excavating these fossils is mere scientific research, that the bones are of no value to them. And that the tribal gods, if they have any, won't be displeased in any way by digging them up. Which I suppose is why they stopped us. Or don't you agree?"

"Well—" Harpirias said.

"Surely the problem was some religious objection, wouldn't you say? We were breaking some kind of taboo?"

"I don't know anything about that. I remind you, I've only just arrived and real negotiations haven't started. What they've asked for, though, is a treaty guaranteeing them that we will refrain forever from any sort of interference in their lives. There's a chance I can at least get back the bones you've already dug up, but I'm not sure that they're going to be willing to allow any additional excavations in the vicinity of their territory."

There was a chorus of immediate objections to that.

"Hold on!" Harpirias said, raising his hands for silence. "Listen to me. I'll do what I can for you. But my main purpose here is simply to get you out of this place, and even that isn't going to be easy. Anything else I happen to achieve in the way of safeguarding past or future scientific research will be strictly a bonus." He glared at them. "Is that understood?"

No one answered.

He chose to take their silence for acquiescence. "Good. Good. Now: aside from the confiscation of the fossils, have you been mistreated in any way that I should be told about?"

"Well," said one of the paleontologists hesitantly, "there's the matter of the women."

Harpirias heard some shushing noises. He saw them exchanging uncomfortable glances.

"The women?" he asked, looking around in bafflement. "What women?"

"This is very embarrassing," Salvinor Hesz said.

"I need to know. What's this about women?"

"They bring us their women," one of the other paleontologists said in the faintest of voices, after a pause that threatened never to end.

"To be fertilized," said another.

"It's the worst part of the whole thing," offered a third. "The absolute worst."

"Shameful."

"Disgraceful."

"Revolting."

Now that they had broken through their reserve, they all

wanted to talk at once. Harpirias faced a confusing babbling clamor of statements, out of which, gradually, he pieced together the story.

Savages though the Othinor might be, apparently they did have some understanding of genetics. They were worried about the negative consequences of tribal inbreeding. As a small group of closely related individuals living as they did in the centuries-long seclusion of their all-but-inaccessible mountain home, they were probably already experiencing plenty of congenital defects. And so they had chosen to regard the arrival of the nine paleontologists as a happy gift of new genetic material. Over the months of the scientists' captivity the Othinor had systematically been sending women into the cave for impregnation. Already, so the paleontologists believed, several halfbreed children had been born, and others were well along the way.

Harpirias's mind swam with outrage and alarm. It began to be clear to him now why a daughter of King Toikella had been waiting for him in his room after the royal banquet.

"This has been going on since the beginning?"

"Since the beginning, yes," Salvinor Hesz said. "Every few days a couple of women are brought here with the regular food delivery and are left here overnight. We're very obviously expected to service them."

"And have you *seen* their women?" demanded Vinin Salal. "Have you *smelled* them? This isn't just moral and physical abuse. It's an esthetic crime!" He trembled with barely contained anger.

Harpirias heard Korinaam snickering. He threw the Shapeshifter a wrathful glance.

Yet it was hard to keep from feeling a certain amusement. In the normal course of things, probably, very few of these dedicated, sober-sided, scholarly men had any more interest in matters of the flesh than he did in digging up fossil bones. For them to be forced to serve as stud males for Othinor women seemed vaguely comic. As for the esthetic issue, well, most of the scientists looked something short of beautiful themselves; nor was their odor, after all these months of captivity, anything of which to boast.

No matter, Harpirias thought. This was no way to treat prisoners. He understood their indignation. He looked at them with deepest sympathy.

"What they have made you do is disgusting," he muttered. "Totally vile."

Vinin Salal said, "The first night, of course, we stayed far away from them. It would never have occurred to us to lay a finger on them. But the next morning they reported what had happened—or rather, hadn't happened—to the guards, and our food that day was withheld. The following morning they came with the food sacks as usual, and there were two new women also. There was a little pantomime. Food: women. Women:

food. We figured out very quickly what we were supposed to do."

"We drew lots," came a voice from the far corner. "The two who got the short straws were elected. And so it has gone ever since."

"But why do you think this is a breeding program?" Harpirias asked. "Maybe the Othinor are just trying to make your imprisonment a little more comfortable for you."

Salvinor Hesz smiled somberly. "Would that that were so. But we know otherwise now. We've learned a smattering of their language, you know, in all this time. The new women coming up tell us about the pregnancies. 'Give me a baby too,' they say. 'Don't send me away empty. The king will be angry with me if I don't conceive.' There's no doubt about it. They sound almost desperate."

"You'll see soon enough," said Vinin Salal. "He'll want you to contribute to their gene pool too. You in particular, with your aristocratic blood. Mark my words, prince. The king will try to make your stay here more—ah—*comfortable*—just as he has done for us. And then what will you do?"

Harpirias smiled. "I'm not the king's prisoner. And soon you won't be either."

9

That evening, not long after Harpirias had completed his descent from the canyon rim, a second mutilated hajbarak was dumped down into the Othinor village. The circumstances were much the same as before. At dusk a bonfire flared suddenly atop the mountain wall—a different sector of it this time—and diminutive figures could be seen outlined against the gathering darkness of the sky, dancing wildly about. Then another big half-butchered beast came tumbling down the mountainside, bouncing heavily and ricocheting from the rocks as it dropped. It landed near the place where the other one had fallen.

The disturbance outside brought Harpirias from his room. He saw the king in a state of high ire, shaking his fist at the mountaintop and roaring streams of angry commands at his warriors. Once again the great animal was dragged out of sight; once again, the plaza was ritually purged of bloodstains. Harpirias heard discordant chanting far into the night.

The negotiating session the next morning did not go well.

Korinaam was ill at ease even before it began. "Have a little forbearance today," the Shapeshifter warned Harpirias as they entered the royal chamber. "He'll be in a foul mood. Don't provoke him in any way. I suggest that you simply express your regrets over this latest shocking death of a sacred hajbarak and request an immediate adjournment of the session."

"Time's wasting, Korinaam. I need to ask him about this monstrous business of forcing the prisoners to sleep with women of the tribe."

"Ask him another day, prince. Please. *Please.*"

"I'll be the judge of that," Harpirias said.

But there was little opportunity for him to define the agenda of the day's talks. The king seemed deeply shaken. Brooding, remote, edgy, he greeted them with little more than a surly growl and a perfunctory wave of his left hand.

Harpirias told the Shapeshifter to open by saying that the ambassador wished to take up certain matters concerning the welfare of the hostages. A calculated risk, Harpirias thought. Korinaam was plainly reluctant, but so far as Harpirias was able to judge, he did as he was told.

Toikella, slouching on his throne, said nothing, only grunted and shrugged.

"Tell him that it has to do with the women who are being sent to them," Harpirias continued. "That I was extremely disturbed to find out that such things were going on. That I have the strongest objection to such things."

"Prince, I implore you—"

"Tell him. Exactly as I instruct you."

Korinaam gave Harpirias a weary nod. He turned toward the king once more and spoke briefly to him.

This time the response was immediate and violent. Toikella's face turned flaming red. He pounded the sides of the throne and snarled almost incoherently. Then, recovering himself, he spoke more calmly with the Shapeshifter, but in a dark imperious way that left no doubt of his simmering anger. And as he continued to speak his tone gradually grew more heated again.

"You see, prince?" asked Korinaam smugly.

"What's he saying?"

"Essentially, that he isn't interested in discussing this topic with you. That the subject isn't negotiable and in any event he thinks you aren't qualified to talk about it. He's using the scornful form of the pronoun *you,* by the way."

"The scornful form?"

"They employ it when they want to cast doubts on the virility of an enemy."

Harpirias felt his own temper rising. "Still clinging to that notion, is he? Well, you can tell him for me—"

"Wait," Korinaam broke in. The king was still speaking.

"He says—we should take ourselves out of his presence at once, he says. No talks at all today. The session is canceled."

"Because he's so upset over the hajbaraks?"

"Not only that. It's much more complicated. He was in a touchy mood to begin with, but you've made it a lot worse, I'm afraid. Just as I warned you. He's worked himself up into a real fit of rage. We have to go, right now."

"You can't mean that. Waste yet another day? It'll be winter here before we ever get down to—"

"We have no choice. If you could understand the things he's saying, you'd know that. Come—come—he'll be throwing pieces of the throne at us in another minute." Korinaam plucked nervously at the sleeve of Harpirias's jerkin. "Come, prince!"

When they were outside Harpirias said, "All right. What was it that sent him up the tree like that?"

"It's the matter of your vow of chastity, prince. That's what is really troubling him, not the hostages or anything else. When you began to talk about the women who are being sent to the hostages, you reminded him of the other thing—your refusing of his daughter."

"My chastity is no concern of his."

"Ah, but it is, it is, prince! Just as you heard yesterday from those men in the ice-cave: he is expecting you to sire a royal heir for him. He is furious because you sent his daughter away, and the talks are not going to make any progress whatever until you embrace her and plant the son of a Coronal in her womb."

"The son of a Coronal!" Harpirias cried. "Is that what he thinks he'll get out of me?"

The Shapeshifter's impenetrable eyes might have been showing a certain sly pleasure. He said nothing.

"For the love of the Divine, Korinaam, do you see what you've done? I told you and told you and told you again that I didn't care for the idea of letting him think that I was Lord Ambinole. I ordered you on at least three different occasions to make the truth known to him. But you refused, and refused, and refused once more, and now—do you see? He wants a Coronal's child for a grandson, and how can I give him that? I am not the Coronal, Korinaam! Not! Not!"

"You are of royal blood, prince."

"A thousand years removed."

"Nevertheless. Your ancestor was a great king. Even if you are not Coronal yourself, we can explain that you are royal. Make the child, and Toikella will be satisfied."

"Make the child?" Harpirias sputtered. "What are you saying?"

"Is it such a dreadful chore? The girl seemed fair enough to me."

Harpirias drew a deep breath. "As if you could tell. But what the girl looks like is completely beside the point. I'm simply not going to— No," he said grimly. "We go back in there and you let him know the truth about who I am, and that's that."

"He will kill us, prince." There was no mockery in the Shapeshifter's tone now.

"Do you mean that?"

"He thinks you are his lordship. It is too late to tell him anything else. He has too much pride invested in having the Coronal of Majipoor as a suppliant in his village. If we tell him at this late hour that we've allowed him to deceive himself about who you really are up till now, he'll kill us both out of hand. Believe me, prince."

"But that would be an act of war! His lordship's government would send an army in here and carry him away into prison for the rest of his life."

"He has no idea of the strength of his lordship's government," Korinaam said. "As you know, he believes that his lordship is a tribal chieftain who is no more important or powerful than he is himself, and that no invader could possibly mount a successful assault on this village. Of course, he would find out eventually that he is wrong. But you and I would still be dead."

Hopeless. Hopeless. Harpirias saw that he was totally boxed in by Korinaam's steadfast refusal to speak the truth to the king and the king's own ill-informed assumptions.

He retreated to his room in the guest house to ponder the situation.

It was wild folly to have let Korinaam sustain this witless

misunderstanding this long. And what a tangle it had become now! To be forced to go on and on with this nonsensical humbuggery, on pain of death, pretending that he was indeed the anointed master of Castle Mount—and to be asked, of all things, to provide the king with an heir in whose veins the royal blood of Majipoor would be combined with that of the Othinor chieftain—

But certainly it was a high crime against the realm to pose as a Coronal. Regardless of the explanations he could give for having undertaken such an imposture, he knew that it was unthinkable to attempt it. And yet—and yet—

Lord Harpirias, Coronal of Majipoor!

He could pretend to it if there was a good reason for doing so, could he not? For the sake of the mission? Conduct himself as though he were king? Stalk around this icy realm of misery as though he were indeed the master of Castle Mount, as though it was he who held the royal seat upon the glorious Confalume Throne, he who wore the starburst crown? How would Toikella ever know it was not so?

No. This was vacuous nonsense.

He could no more imagine himself to be Coronal than he could imagine himself old. He was Harpirias of Muldemar, a young man of the Prestimion line, a minor prince of the Castle Mount aristocracy. He wanted to go on being Harpirias of Muldemar. He was satisfied with that. He had no ambitions beyond that. To masquerade, even here, even for a moment, even out of supposed diplomatic necessity, as the lord of the world would be a grotesque blasphemy.

He knew he must correct the foolishness into which Korinaam had thrust him before it proceeded any further.

But how?

No answer presented itself. Harpirias was still puzzling over it, alone in his room, far into the evening.

Then, very late, came a voice at his door, a woman's voice, speaking softly to him in words he was unable to understand.

"Who is it?" he called. But he had a good idea.

She spoke again. There seemed to be a plaintive, imploring note in her voice.

Harpirias went to the door, pulled the leather flap aside. Yes, it was she: the one who had come to him before, the king's young dark-haired daughter. Tonight she was more formally dressed, a fine robe of white fur, leather buskins, a bright scarlet ribbon elaborately woven through the glossy bowl of her hair. A spindle-shaped sliver of carved bone had been thrust into her upper lip from side to side: some sort of tribal jewelry, no doubt.

She looked terrified. Her eyes were wide and rigidly fixed on him, and she was trembling in a way that had nothing to do with the chill of the air. A muscle was jerking rhythmically in her cheek. Harpirias stood there a long while, staring at her, not knowing what to do.

"No," he said to her after a time, trying to keep his voice

gentle. "I'm really sorry. But I can't do this. I simply can't." He smiled sadly, shook his head, pointed outward through the door. "Can you understand what I'm saying? You have to go. What you want from me is something I can't give you."

She shivered in an almost convulsive way. Held out her hands to him. They were shaking.

"No," she said, and to his amazement she was speaking his language. "No—please—please—"

"You know Majipoori?"

Not very much of it, apparently. He had the impression that the girl was speaking by rote. "Please—please—I—come—in?—"

Korinaam has taught her this, Harpirias thought suddenly. That would be very much like him.

He shook his head again.

"You can't. You mustn't. I'm simply not going to—"

"Please!" There was a terrible urgency in her tone. She seemed about to fall at his feet.

In the face of that, how could he turn her away? Harpirias sighed and beckoned her in. Just for a little while, he told himself. A little while, and that would be all.

The girl stumbled into the icy room. It was impossible for her to stop shivering. Harpirias wanted to put his arms around her and offer comfort. But he could not allow himself to do that. It was important to keep his distance.

Evidently she had exhausted her few comprehensible

words now. She was gesturing to him in some sort of pantomime, raising her arms high over her head and bringing them down to her sides in a broad sweeping gesture, then doing it again, again, again. Harpirias struggled to make sense out of her miming. Something big. A mountain, was that what she was portraying? Did this have anything to do with the two dead animals that had been thrown down into the village from the top of the canyon wall?

She swept one hand downward in front of herself in a swelling curve from her forehead to her knees. Indicating her belly? A representation of the pregnancy that she desired from him? Maybe not. She made the mountain gesture again, and then the belly. He watched her uncomprehendingly. She opened her mouth, pointed to her teeth. The mountain again. The belly. Once more the teeth.

Harpirias shook his head.

She paused in thought for an instant or two. Then she thrust her arms out toward the floor at an angle, a gesture that seemed to indicate size, and began to march stiff-leggedly around the room in a comical hulking way.

He was altogether lost. "An animal? A big animal? A hajbarak?"

"No. No." She looked annoyed at his denseness. Once more the mountain, the belly, the teeth. The hulking stiff-legged strut. And this time he got it.

A mountain that walked—a big belly—and the teeth—a big potbellied man with unusual teeth—

"Toikella!" he cried.

The girl nodded happily. Comprehension at last.

He waited. She appeared to be thinking again. Then, as she had done the last time she had come to him, she pointed toward the pile of sleeping-furs, tapped her chest, extended her hand to Harpirias. Harpirias began to explain to her once again that he wasn't willing to go to bed with her. But before he could say anything she acted out the Toikella pantomime again; and then she let her face puff up and her eyes turn demented in what was clearly a representation of royal anger, and went jumping around the room furiously wielding an imaginary sword or lance. After which, shrinking down from her Toikella size to her own, she clutched at her body with both her arms and made her eyes glaze over. Wounded. Dying.

"Toikella will kill you if I don't sleep with you?" Harpirias asked. "Is that it?"

She gave him a helpless uncomprehending look. He tried again, speaking louder and more slowly. "King—will—kill—you?"

The girl shrugged and went through the whole pantomimed rigmarole again.

"Kill both of us?" Harpirias asked. "Kill only me?"

But words were useless. Evidently she had already uttered

every word of his language that she understood, all four or five of them. He knew only two or three words of hers, and none that would help him now.

She was imploring him with her eyes. Looking desperately at him, then looking toward the pile of furs. Offering herself to him once more.

Harpirias realized that he had probably caught the gist of her anguished charade correctly. Her father the king had ordered her to bear a royal heir. He would settle for nothing less. If Harpirias sent her away as he had before, Toikella's ire would be aroused to a murderous heat.

Whether it was the girl that he would kill, or Harpirias, or the two of them, was not something that he had been able to get from her. But it made no difference. The implications were clear that some sort of violence would come from this, unless he yielded to the king's blind insistence.

And, trapped between the cynical lies that Korinaam had told and the dynastic expectations of King Toikella, Harpirias saw that he had no choice.

"All right," he said to her. "Come on. I'll make a little prince for you, if that's what your father wants so badly."

He didn't expect her to understand anything of that, nor did she. But when he caught her lightly by the wrist and drew her toward the bed of furs her eyes brightened in immediate comprehension. A kind of glow came into her face that made her seem almost attractive.

Not that she was particularly repugnant, Harpirias thought. Stockier and more muscular than he really preferred a woman to be, and somewhat deficient in bodily cleanliness, perhaps, and the dark spaces in her smile where front teeth were missing disturbed him. But—even so—

He had never been an outstanding model of moral fastidiousness himself. In his time Harpirias had embraced more than a few young women whose deportment and appearance would have raised eyebrows at the Coronal's court. That laughing red-haired dancing girl long ago in Bombifale, the one with the fiery eyes and the hoarse shrill voice of a fish-peddler—and that slim-legged juggler lass in the holiday town of High Morpin, who could swear like a sailor—and especially that swaggering broad-hipped huntress he had met while wandering alone in the forests back of Normork, who had showed him a trick or two when he was eighteen that would never have crossed his mind—

There had been others. More than a few, more than a few. If he was forced now to add a swarthy smudge-faced barbarian girl to the list, well, so be it. Diplomats have to perform all sorts of unusual things in the course of their duties, Harpirias told himself once again. His mission would very likely fail if he persisted in his prissy refusal to honor Toikella's wishes in this matter. Therefore it could be construed as his professional duty to oblige the king. And if he was not in fact the Coronal, for all that Toikella had chosen to believe he was, it was certainly true that the blood of Coronals past ran in his veins. The king would have to be satisfied with that.

So be it. So be it.

Harpirias unfastened the robe of white fur and held it open as the girl slipped out of it.

She was naked beneath it. Her body was lean and taut-fleshed, with small hard breasts and nicely flaring hips. Apparently she had oiled herself from head to foot with something—could it be hajbarak grease, he wondered?—that gave her a smooth and agreeably slippery feel, and masked to some extent the scent of her unwashed skin.

They dropped down together to the pile of hides. Harpirias quickly wriggled into the middle of the heap, for it was much too cold in the ice-walled room for him to want to expose his unclothed body very long to the air. Though apparently the girl would have preferred to remain on top of the pile rather than within it, she seemed to understand his need, and after a bit she followed him underneath. Once they were safely covered, side by side and snug beneath the mound of furs, she laughed and pressed her hand against his chest, rolling over and pushing him down so that she could climb into the upper position.

"That's how you like it, is it? Fine. Whatever you want."

She grinned down at him. There was a playful sparkle in her eyes, as though this were some sort of game for her. Harpirias wondered how old she was. Twenty? Younger, maybe. Fifteen? There was no telling.

He tried to kiss her, but she averted her mouth. Not their custom, apparently. So be it, Harpirias thought. That little sliver of carved bone stuck through her upper lip would have caused difficulties anyway.

She said something to him in her language. "I don't understand," he told her. She laughed and said it again. Othinor words of tender passion? Somehow he doubted that. Maybe she was just telling him her name.

"Harpirias," he said. "My name is Harpirias. What's yours?"

She giggled. Said something again, a single word, which a moment later she said a second time. Perhaps it was of some significance; but of course, he hadn't a clue to its meaning.

"Shabilikat?" he ventured.

His attempt at mimicking her sent the girl into a gale of wild laughter.

"Shabilikat," he said again. "Shabilikat."

It seemed to amuse her inordinately to hear him repeating the word. But when he tried it one more time she put her hand over his mouth; and then, an instant later, she wrapped her powerful thighs around his waist, straddling him in a manner that left him without much of an urge to make further attempts at conversation.

It was a long night, and an active one, and rather more pleasant than Harpirias had anticipated, although the style of it was very strange to a man accustomed to the more polished women of the Majipoor aristocracy. Yet he accommodated readily enough to the lusty vigor of her lovemaking, the eager clawing hands, the fierce rocking thrusts, the robust uproarious outbursts of hilarity at what struck him as oddly inopportune moments. She seemed insatiable. Harpirias, though, after long months of unbroken continence, was far from troubled by that.

Somewhere along the way the furs with which he had covered them went flying to one side, but he hardly noticed the cold. Eventually—he had no idea how many hours later it was—he tumbled suddenly into the deepest and darkest of sleeps, the way one might tumble into a well; and when he woke, much later, he discovered that she had covered him once again while he slept and had slipped out of his room without awakening him.

He could not know, naturally, whether he had indeed sired a little princeling for Toikella on her that night. But if the effort had been a failure, he told himself, well, then, he would be quite willing to make another try at it.

10

The king, the next day, was in a far more congenial mood than he had been yesterday. He greeted Harpirias at the entrance to the throne chamber with hugs and bellows of hearty affection, and then with lascivious grins and winks and sniggers and nudges that made Harpirias wince with barely concealed embarrassment. Plainly Toikella had had a full report from the girl and had been very much pleased by what he heard.

But he still refused to let Harpirias draw him into any specific negotiations. He was in truth, as Korinaam had said, a man who disliked being hurried.

Harpirias had the Shapeshifter deliver a tactfully worded request for a discussion of the welfare of the hostages. Toikella's reply was cool and brief, and even Harpirias could tell that it was a refusal.

He looked toward Korinaam. "He says no, does he?"

"The king wishes to assure you that all will be well in regard to everything you wish, but he asserts that this is not the time to talk about it. He is going to set out on a hunting trip three days hence and it would be unlucky for him to engage in matters of any substance until he returns."

"Which will be how long? A week? A month?"

"Two days. One to ascend, one to return. Perhaps a third day if the animals make themselves scarce."

"By the Lady! If this keeps up we're *never* going to—"

"You are invited to accompany him," Korinaam continued smoothly. "I advise that you accept. The midsummer royal hunt is a great sacred festival of these people, and he is honoring you greatly by asking you to come."

"Well, then," Harpirias said, somewhat mollified. But all this delay was irksome to him none the less.

The rest of that morning's meeting was devoted to plans for the trip. Afterward, as he and Korinaam were returning to their lodging house, Harpirias said, "You taught that girl how to say words like 'please' and 'I come in,' didn't you?"

"I felt that the situation was dangerous. She needed my help."

"Dangerous to whom?"

"The king was very resentful of her failure to seduce you that first night. He saw it as something close to treason on her part. It is always dangerous to attract the resentment of a barbarian king."

"And you think he would have had her killed if I hadn't allowed her to—"

"There was that possibility. It seemed wisest to me not to risk it. The king was determined to have his way. He would only have sent another woman to you if this one hadn't succeeded."

"No doubt you're right," said Harpirias. Then, when they had walked on a few steps, something else crossed his mind and he asked the Metamorph, "Do you happen to know the meaning of the Othinor word 'shabilikat'?"

"What?"

" 'Shabilikat,' " Harpirias repeated. "Or something approximately like that. It's a word that she spoke just as she and I were—were about to—"

"Say it again."

Harpirias pronounced it once more, clearly, carefully. Korinaam was slow to respond. Then he began to laugh, not a familiar thing coming from him. The laughter began as a quiet inward sound but quickly grew to a guffaw.

"So it's funny, is it?"

"Obscene, actually. So—terribly—filthy—" Korinaam appeared positively electrified by the word. "Of course you're mispronouncing it hideously. It's more like—" And he delivered himself of something that had the same number of syllables, but was studded with an impossible array of jaw-cracking consonants heaped together like boulders. "Is that more like what she actually said?"

"I suppose. What does it mean?"

Korinaam hesitated. He was snickering in a way that made Harpirias want to smack him across his face. "I can't say it out loud. It's too awful."

"Come on. You're not a child, Korinaam. Don't be coy with me!"

"I ask you, prince—"

"And I order you."

"Knowledge of this word is not essential to your diplomatic work."

"How can you be sure of that? I want you to tell me what it means."

Korinaam's forehead was chartreuse with embarrassment. He smothered an attack of the titters and said, forcing the words out with no little difficulty, "It means—roughly—'The gateway of my body is open to you.' Feminine mode of address to masculine listener. Men and women use different verb forms here."

Harpirias understood now why the girl had been so amused when he had repeated the word to her. It was a simple grammatical error, a man using the feminine form of speech. But where was the filth that Korinaam saw in the word? The gateway of her body *was* open. She was simply describing the situation as it existed at that moment. If he had unknowingly used the wrong verb form when he had repeated what she had said, well, no one could have expected him to understand the subtleties of Othinor grammar.

He gave the Shapeshifter a perplexed look. Korinaam had his head turned away from him and was staring abashedly at the ground.

"I don't find anything obscene in that phrase," he said. "Erotic, maybe, yes, but not obscene."

"The image—the body perceived as having a gateway—" Korinaam was unable to go on.

"But it does. The female body, anyway. Explain to me why anybody—particularly a savage like her, uncomplicated, uncorrupted by civilization's absurdities—would see obscenity in a straightforwardly anatomical descriptive metaphor?"

"She probably doesn't," said Korinaam. Harpirias had never seen him look so uncomfortable. "*I* do. —If we may, prince, may we speak of something else?"

Once more Harpirias was reminded of how very alien his traveling companion actually was. They might have political equality everywhere on Majipoor, yes; their queen was officially regarded as a Power of the Realm, and all that; but nevertheless they were different, different in unknowable ways, a race whose strange pliant bodies functioned along principles unique to themselves and whose minds—whose minds, Harpirias thought, were capable of regarding the simple notion that the female body has an entrance as a vile obscenity.

How did Metamorphs make love? he wondered.

Harpirias realized that he didn't know. And didn't want to find out.

He parted from Korinaam outside the lodging house and stood for a while in the plaza, looking up at the sky. It had turned a dark metallic gray, like a sheet of cold iron. A few whirling snowflakes floated overhead.

A storm was coming on; it was starting to snow; and yet this was the eve of the midsummer hunting festival! As he watched, the force of the snowfall increased appreciably. Already a thin white dusting had begun to cover the old and darkened ice of the plaza floor. Midsummer! Midsummer! Harpirias felt the hard little flakes striking his upturned cheeks. How strange this all is, he thought. Wherever he turned he found himself amidst strangenesses. He would have quite a story to tell, if ever he returned from this place.

The girl came to him again that night. The snow had stopped by then, after a considerable fall. Boys with brooms of straw were out in the plaza, clearing the places where high drifts were blocking access to doorways.

Harpirias had found out from Korinaam at dinnertime how to say "What is your name?" in the Othinor language, and he asked it of her when she arrived.

"Ivla Yevikenik," she told him.

He pointed to her and repeated it. She nodded and tapped her breast. "Ivla Yevikenik," she said again.

"Harpirias," he said, pointing to himself.

"Harpirias."

So they had that much established, at least.

She seemed to think that because he could speak one sentence in her language, he now was completely fluent in it. A torrent of baffling chatter came from her; and he ended it only by laughing and hitting the side of his head with his fingertips, as though to say that there was nothing but emptiness inside. She appeared to understand that. But she wanted to talk, even so. For a long while they struggled to communicate, each laboriously explaining words to the other, without accomplishing anything; and then at last they gave up and headed toward the pile of furs.

She murmured the word that he heard as "Shabilikat" again, just as Harpirias was about to enter her. He did not repeat it this time.

Afterward, when they lay naked and panting together waiting for his strength to reassert itself, she began to speak again to him, softly, almost tenderly. Phrases of endearment, he supposed. Or, perhaps, gratitude for his willingness to surrender to Toikella's requirements. That made Harpirias a little uneasy. Her gratitude was not what he wanted.

The girl is actually quite attractive, he told himself. I am not doing this as a favor to anybody but myself.

Was that true? Not really, he knew. But he wished very much to feel that it was.

In the middle of the night she insisted on going out into the plaza with him. Which seemed crazy to him, but there was no doubt of her meaning, for she arose and dressed herself, and held his clothing out to him with a clear indication that he should put it on, and then took him by the hand and led him from the building.

All was silent outside. The night was clear and cold, with three small moons in the sky and a brilliant sprinkling of stars. She began to tell him something in pantomime, the same set of gestures over and over, pointing to the canyon wall and then going up on tiptoes as if pointing over it, and gradually Harpirias divined that she wanted him to describe the world beyond that great stone wall for her.

One of the brooms with which the boys had been sweeping the plaza lay discarded nearby. He picked it up and used the end of its handle to inscribe a map of Majipoor in the newly fallen snow, the two main continents side by side with the Isle of the Lady between them and the sun-cursed desert continent of Suvrael below.

Did she understand what he had drawn? How could he tell?

"This is where we are," he said, pointing with the broom handle to the northeastern tip of Zimroel and speaking with exaggerated precision, as though that would help her understand. "The Khyntor Marches, we call this region." He glanced at her to see if the name had registered; but her face showed only intense curiosity, no comprehension. He pushed up a ridge of snow to indicate the mountain range that cut the Marches off from the rest of the western continent.

"Down here," he said, "this is the city of Ni-moya. Big, big, *big* city. Many, many millions of people." He felt like an idiot, speaking to her this way. He sketched in the River Zimr, running from west to east across the upper third of the continent, and poked the handle into the snow at the river's mouth to mark the city of Piliplok. "Seaport," he said. "Very big. Lots of Skandars live here." Harpirias tried to demonstrate the concept of having four arms. "*Skan-dars.* And this river here, running up from the south—that's the Steiche. Metamorphs live here, in the jungles. You can't imagine what a jungle is, can you? Very hot. Rain all the time. Huge trees. That's where the Metamorphs come from. People like Korinaam. *Meta-morphs. Kori-naam.*"

Useless. Preposterous.

But she encouraged him with nods and eager grins to go on. He drew in more of the major cities of Zimroel for her, as well as he could remember them from his school days, Pidruid and Til-omon and Narabal over on the western coast, and Dulorn more or less where it belonged inland, and a few more. Then he moved over to the other great circle he had drawn, the one representing the continent of Alhanroel, and knelt in the snow, reaching his arms out to swoop up a heap of it that would stand for Castle Mount.

"This is where I live," he said. "Big, big mountain, *this* high, tremendous mountain reaching to the stars, cities all around its sides. Castle on top. *Cas-tle.* The castle of the Coronal. *Coro-nal.* King of the world. Lord Ambinole, the Coronal of Majipoor."

He was beginning to freeze, now, on this fine summer night. His ears and the tip of his nose were burning. But he was determined not to abandon this geography lesson so long as she was paying attention, and Ivla Yevikenik was definitely paying attention, staring at him in a rapt, captivated way. Harpirias poked with the broom for her again and again, drawing the River Glayge with the Labyrinth of the Pontifex at its southern end, the cities of Alaisor and Treynone and Stoien, and the ancient stone ruins that had once been the Metamorph capital, Velalisier. And would have gone on until morning, naming all that there was to name, every one of the Fifty Cities and much else besides, except that after a few minutes more she came up beside him and rubbed her cheek against his shoulder. She had had enough geography for now.

"Shabilikat," she said, and led him inside.

11

The trail to the sacred hunting grounds began right behind the royal palace and rose in five sharp switchbacks to a deep lateral crevice in the mountain wall that was invisible from below; and from there it wound gradually back and forth, up and up, until the canyon rim came into view. The path was much like the one to the cave where the hostages were being kept, rough and rocky and narrow, but not quite as steep. Harpirias found it far less of a challenge, although the snow of a few days before, still mostly unmelted, made the going trickier than it might otherwise have been.

The hunting party had twelve members. Toikella led the way, with the high priest Mankhelm beside him, followed by six husky villagers carrying hunting gear and some sort of holy regalia in a painted wooden box. Harpirias had Korinaam with him to serve as interpreter, and had been permitted also to bring two of the Skandars, presumably as porters, though there was nothing for them to carry.

This part of the canyon rim was higher and more irregular than the one Harpirias had visited earlier. Instead of terminating in a flat broad summit, it appeared to lead to a series of even higher ridges beyond, stretching on and on to the north—a jagged sloping plateau of sorts, no doubt the grazing grounds for the beasts that the king had come here to hunt.

They halted a long while at the transitional point of the canyon wall proper, where it ceased to rise in a straight vertical line but leveled off before beginning its next uneven swoop northward. The village could still be seen from here—just barely, far below—but it would be hidden from view beyond this point.

Here the king stripped off his robes and stood naked, evidently untroubled by the cold, silently looking on while Mankhelm performed a long series of rituals. The priest solemnly arranged twigs and bits of dried grass and scraps of colored leather in patterns on the ground and set fire to them; he built three little cairns of pebbles and muttered words into them; he opened a jug of beer or perhaps some stronger liquor and offered splashes of it to the four quarters of the horizon.

The climax of the rite came when one of the bearers undid a fur blanket that was tied with a thick leather cord, and drew from it a spear of astonishing length and heft that was tipped with a great triangular point of some glassy-looking white stone chipped to razor sharpness. He handed the huge weapon to Mankhelm, who formally raised it aloft with both hands and passed it over to Toikella. As Harpirias looked on in amazement the naked king brandished the mighty spear high over his head, shook it fiercely three times as if he meant to intimidate the gods with it, and delivered himself of a long rumbling war-whoop which reverberated through the mountains with such force that Harpirias expected boulders and whole crags to come crashing down around them.

And this is Majipoor, Harpirias thought, in the thirteenth year of the Pontificate of Taghin Gawad!

The echo of Toikella's cry died away. The king resumed his robe; the bearers picked up the ceremonial spear and returned it to its fur wrap; the high priest Mankhelm kicked his pebble cairns apart and ground his foot into the charred bits of twigs and grass. Whatever rite had been observed here was done. They were ready, it seemed, to proceed now with the royal hunt itself.

"Look there," Eskenazo Marabaud said.

The Skandar was pointing toward a distant high ridge. Harpirias shaded his eyes against the glare of the sky, but his eyes were not as keen as Eskenazo Marabaud's and he could make out nothing unusual up there.

King Toikella, though, who also had followed the Skandar's pointing arm, evidently could. He had taken up a peculiar fixed stance, legs far apart, head thrown back, and was studying the ridge in rigid concentration. After a moment a long thick strangled sound of rage came from his throat.

"What do you see?" Harpirias asked Eskenazo Marabaud.

"Figures. Moving about, right at the top."

"I don't see them."

"Look harder, then, prince. There. There, coming down that ridge."

Harpirias stared. All he saw was tumbled masses of rock. He glanced sideways at Korinaam. The Shapeshifter was looking toward the high ridge in the same intent way as the king, and he was trembling. His hands were knotted together tensely behind his back and his arms from shoulder to wrist were writhing and rippling like a couple of agitated serpents.

Then at last Harpirias made out what the others were seeing: a dark line of diminutive figures, perhaps eight or ten of them, emerging like evil gnomes from sheltered crannies in the fissured rock of the ridge and clambering up toward a kind of natural amphitheater just below the highest point. It was easier to see them there. They were long-limbed, slender, almost spidery of build—very different in appearance from the thick-set Othinor.

Toikella shook both his clenched fists at them and grunted something.

"What is he saying?" Harpirias asked Korinaam.

"He says, 'Enemies—enemies—' "

"The ones who threw the dead hajbaraks into the village, do you think?"

"It could be," the Shapeshifter said. "How should I know?" His voice was faint and remote, and he spoke without taking his eyes from the figures on the heights. His hands still were locked together behind his back and he had not stopped trembling.

Now the enraged king broke from his stasis. Gesturing to the other Othinor to follow him, he launched into a wild upward scramble. There was no longer any kind of path here, only a wide sloping apron covered with rocks and pebbles and the occasional boulder. Toikella, lurching and clawing and scrabbling, slithering up through shallow openings in the rock and often tumbling back down again, moved like a man possessed by dark spirits. It was as though he meant to seize the trespassers with his bare hands and hurl them from the mountain. Mankhelm and the Othinor bearers struggled upward after him, not far behind.

Harpirias had no choice but to climb with them. It would be distinctly unwise to let himself become separated from the royal party in these mountains.

When he had ascended a hundred paces or so, he looked back and saw that Korinaam had not accompanied him. The Metamorph still stood motionless below, like one who was lost in dreams, peering up at the figures on the far-off ridge.

Angrily Harpirias called to him. "Korinaam? Korinaam! Stay close to me!"

"Yes—I'm coming—coming—"

Harpirias waited for him to catch up. The Skandars had already gone ahead.

He had a better view of the creatures on the upper ridge from here. They were arrayed in a straight line right along the top now, and had gone into a madcap dance, tipping their heads from side to side, waggling their long slender arms, kicking their knees high: a frantic devil-dance of obvious derision and scorn. They were defying Toikella to come and get them.

But Toikella had no hope of getting to them. When he had climbed a little farther Harpirias saw that a steep hidden declivity separated this ridge from the higher one. Toikella and his men had reached it and gone down into it, but from the looks of that sudden slope they would need all day to descend one side of it and come up the other. Their quarry was unlikely to wait for them.

And in fact the Othinor were coming back already. Somber-faced, weary-looking, they moved slowly into view, their heads and then their shoulders and their bodies becoming visible as they rose up out of the chasm.

Harpirias looked up again toward the dancers on the heights. They were gone, or so it seemed to him at first; but then he caught a glimpse of them off toward the left, clearly outlined against the bright sky as they went scampering away over the sharp spine of the ridge.

What was this, though? He felt certain that they were running on all four legs, as wolves would do. And yet just a moment before they had looked unmistakably human in form.

A band of Shapeshifters? Here?

"What do you say, Korinaam? Are those some of your people? What would Piurivars be doing living in these mountains?"

But Korinaam only shrugged and shook his head, and made no other answer. The identity of the creatures on the ridge was apparently a matter of complete indifference to him just now. He looked exhausted by the climb. His eyes were glazed, his narrow shoulders were slumped, his breath came in short rasping bursts.

In the succeeding hours there were no additional sightings of the mysterious creatures of the heights. They had appeared, they had done their mocking dance, they had vanished. But the strange episode cast a long shadow over the royal hunt all the rest of that day. Toikella stalked ahead in frosty silence, striding up one ridge and down the next, lost in a private realm of angry brooding. Nor did any of the other Othinor speak a word. Accompanied by Korinaam and the Skandars, Harpirias trailed along behind them, understanding nothing of what had taken place.

Animals could be seen in the flatlands between the crests—black shaggy things, seemingly of great size, ambling slowly over the rocky plains and nibbling at the sparse patches of stubby gray-green grass. Hajbaraks, were they? Korinaam was unsure and the Othinor still remained grimly uncommunicative. In any case the beasts were well beyond range, and drifted even farther away as Toikella approached them.

The air grew cooler as the day went along: there was a real bite in it now. The bleak upland terrain was gray and cheerless. Harpirias felt his spirits sagging ever deeper from hour to hour. This was nothing like the hunts he had known on Castle Mount. Those had been joyous sport, this was a dismal dreary trek.

It began to appear likely that the sacred hunt would last several days, or perhaps even more. That was a gloomy prospect indeed.

Toward evening, though, some unwary animal unexpectedly came rushing out from between two vertical slabs of pink rock, right into the midst of the hunting party. It was a scruffy-looking gray beast of only moderate size, big-headed and lean, with unpleasant curving claws and a long slavering mouth: a scavenger of some sort, from the looks of it. One of the king's manservants began to swing at it with the staff he was carrying, as if to swat it aside like vermin; but Toikella let out a great raging cry and quickly stepped forward. Catching the staff in mid-course and twisting it from the man's hand, the king roughly shoved the servant down and out of his way. Then he drew the short sword that he wore on a thong around his waist and thrust it into the befuddled animal's belly.

The wounded beast reared back, rising up on its back legs

and striking ineffectually at Toikella with its curved claws. The king brushed the animal's forearm aside in the most casual way and thrust again, and a third time; and the creature uttered a soft bubbling sigh and fell down on its side. Streams of greenish-red blood came in spurting gushes from its wounds.

The king said a few curt words to Mankhelm. Immediately the priest drew a flask of black leather from his box of holy regalia and held it to the gouts of spouting blood until it was full. He handed it then to the king; and then, kneeling, Mankhelm began to flay the dying animal even as it slowly threshed about.

"What's happening?" Harpirias asked Korinaam in a low voice.

"I'm not certain. But it's a ritual butchering of some sort, that much is clear."

"Isn't the king supposed to be hunting hajbaraks on this expedition?"

"Perhaps he's decided that this animal will do."

And indeed that seemed to be the case. The priest had now laid the animal's flesh bare—it was dead, finally—and with the efficiency of one who has long been accustomed to preparing sacrificial offerings he was cutting the thing into sections, laying the meat of the haunches over here, the heart nearby, certain other of the internal organs in a different place. Harpirias had to admire Mankhelm's skill at stripping and quartering the creature. When the job was done the priest rose and draped the animal's raw moist skin over Toikella's broad shoulders, fastening it in place with a beaded leather cord that he tied about the king's neck. The head of the beast, still attached to the hide, dangled down along the royal back, dead eyes glassily staring outward.

What followed was shocking even to someone as experienced in the bloodshed of the hunt as Harpirias. Toikella held the black leather flask of blood aloft, solemnly offering it to the four quarters of the heavens; and then he drank it down in four or five gulps. Next he knelt and devoured the red and steaming heart. Something that was probably the liver he handed to Mankhelm, who consumed part of it and set the remainder atop a flat rock that had evidently been chosen to serve as an altar. The rest of the meat the king divided, giving torn bloody segments to each of his men, and then turning toward Harpirias with one for him.

Harpirias stared blankly.

"Take it," Korinaam whispered. "Eat it."

"But it's *raw.*"

The Shapeshifter glared at him. "You're being asked to participate in one of the holiest rituals these people have. Perhaps the holiest. The king is paying you a high compliment. Take it. Eat it."

Harpirias gave him a morose nod.

Tembidat, he thought, *you will owe me much for all this!*

The meat was hard and stringy, and its flavor was that of

dead things. Somehow Harpirias choked it down, though he came close to vomiting. Toikella watched in evident satisfaction as Harpirias swallowed it, and clapped him lustily between the shoulderblades when he was done.

The others in Harpirias's party were spared the honor of partaking of the holy meat. None of them appeared to be unhappy about that.

There was chanting now, and a ceremonial burning of the uneaten parts of the animal's body. The rest of the carcass was simply tossed down the closest ravine. Then the king spoke briefly to his men, who began at once to pack and stow the hunting gear.

"Is that it?" Harpirias asked. "The hunt is over?"

"So the king has decreed," said the Shapeshifter. "He's not going to bother going after a hajbarak. This animal has been designated the official midsummer sacrifice and this year's hunt is at its end."

"He's upset about the people he saw dancing on the ridge, isn't he? That's why he's cutting things short."

"Very likely."

"Who were they, Korinaam? *What* were they?"

"I have no idea," the Metamorph said tightly. He looked away. The question seemed to pain him. "Ah: we're just about ready to leave, it would appear. We're going to go back down to the village now."

"Now? But it's starting to get dark!"

"Nevertheless, we seem to be leaving."

There could be no doubt about that. Already the towering figure of King Toikella, still clad in the bloody animal skin, was a good distance along the way, heading back toward the place where the trail down to the village began. Harpirias had no choice but to fall in with the marchers, though the dusk was deepening rapidly now into night and it struck him as perilous in the extreme to attempt the icy, rock-strewn path at this late hour. Would they even reach the trail at all before full darkness came? Or would they have to go blundering through the broken and difficult terrain of this plateau without being able to see where they were going?

He hurried to catch up with the swiftly striding Othinor.

No one said so much as a word during the downward march. The king's mood was so black that his men gave him a wide berth. Beyond any question the hunt had been something far short of a success, even if Toikella had chosen to decree that it was.

The descent, illuminated only by the light of one crescent moon, was a slow and harrowing one. The trail was all but invisible; it could only have been by instinct alone that Toikella chose the right path out of the myriad dimly seen choices that presented themselves. Somewhere in the middle of the night a cold harsh wind slicing downward from the summit began to blow against their backs. Harpirias wondered if the wild gusts would sweep them from the trail and fling them down the side of the mountain, their bodies tumbling into the plaza of the village like those of the murdered hajbaraks. He shivered and huddled into himself and placed his feet with exaggerated care at every step.

It was dawn before they reached the bottom of the canyon wall. Exhausted by the night's exertions, Harpirias went straight to his room and buried himself beneath the entire pile of furs.

As he settled in he wondered once more what those creatures were who had jeered and mocked the king of the Othinor on that high ridge. Surely they were the same who had slain the royal beasts and hurled their bodies to the canyon floor. Something very strange was happening here: but what? What?

He had no answers. Whatever mystery was unfolding among these people, he was without any way of penetrating it.

Even under the furs Harpirias could not stop shivering. The morning sounds of the awakening village came dimly to him through the ice walls of the guest lodge. But neither the cold nor the noise mattered to him for long. He was governed now by fatigue. He drew his knees to his chest and shut his eyes tightly and within moments he went toppling into the deepest of sleep.

12

Immediately upon his return from the high country Harpirias applied himself to the task of learning to speak the language of the Othinor. There was too much going on in this place that was opaque to him; and the only interpreter that he had had shown himself to be untrustworthy. He needed to master the language himself, if he could.

He had never given much thought before to the problem of learning to speak another language. Except in these mountains, Majipoori was universally understood all over the world, and there was no need for a prince of the Mount to trouble himself to become familiar with the tongues that the Vroons, or the Skandars, or the Liimen, or any of the other alien minority races of the planet, might speak among themselves.

Ivla Yevikenik did her best to help him. It was like a game for her, one more amusing thing that they could do together between bouts of lovemaking. There was an air of childish glee about her during their sessions of linguistic studies. She might have a woman's body, Harpirias realized, but in truth she was only a girl, and a simple-hearted one at that. Probably she regarded him as some interesting kind of life-sized doll that her father had chosen to bestow on her. And teaching Harpirias to speak Othinor was just another way of playing with her new toy.

Progress was slow at first. She was able quickly enough to teach Harpirias a few rudimentary things, "hand" and "eye" and "mouth" and other such obvious point-and-ask nouns. But it was not an easy thing for him to go beyond that degree of complexity with her. After a time, though, things began to fit together in his mind in a logical and orderly way; and then, to his surprise and pleasure, Harpirias found himself quickly learning the main elements of the language.

Even now, the grammar remained an enigma to him, and his pronunciation of most words was so far off the mark that it sent her into merry convulsions. But he pieced together enough of a vocabulary so that in short order he was able to communicate with her, after a fashion, through a mixture of half-garbled words, strenuous gestures, and elaborate pantomiming.

Once more he spoke to her of Majipoor, its glories and splendors. Ivla Yevikenik seemed to comprehend much more this time. She scarcely appeared to breathe as he described the world beyond the ice-barrier for her. Her eyes widened in wonder—and, perhaps, disbelief—when he told her of Castle

Mount and its Fifty Cities, High Morpin with its mirror-slides and juggernauts, Halanx and its grand estates, Normork of the great stone wall and the mighty Dekkeret Gate, and high above everything else the ancient Castle of Lord Ambinole in all its unreckonable thousands of rooms, spreading like some huge many-tentacled creature over the summit of the Mount. He told her too of the vastness of the River Zimr, a river the size of an ocean, and of its innumerable towns, Belka and Clarischanz and Gourkaine, Semirod and Impemond and Haunfort Major and all the rest, and also of the place where the Zimr merged with its sister river, the Steiche, to form the enormous inland sea along whose immeasurable shores the city of Ni-moya of the white towers had been built.

Harpirias felt a pang of homesickness as he spoke the names of these places and sights—even the names of cities that he himself had never beheld, even the name of Ni-moya, which he had loathed. For they were all Majipoor, whether he had been to them or not; and he felt hopelessly cut off from the Majipoor he had known in this stark and forlorn land of ice, try as he might to convince himself that this was Majipoor too.

When he had talked with her of Majipoor long enough so that they were starting to grow easier of speech with one another, he asked her about the figures that they had seen on the high ridge, and of her father's angry reaction to their derisive posturing and dancing.

"Who are they?" Harpirias asked. "Do you know?"

"Devils, they are. Wild people. They live beside the Frozen Sea."

In the northernmost reaches of the Khyntor Marches, was what she meant—almost at the planetary pole. The extreme limit of the world, the very brink of nowhere. A place where, according to myth and the ancient conjecture of geographers, the ocean itself had turned to a sheet of perpetual ice and human life was impossible to sustain.

"What kind of people, Ivla Yevikenik? Do they look like us?"

"No."

"What, then?"

She groped for words, could not find useful ones, and instead began to move around the room in an odd sideways manner, holding her shoulders hunched together and her arms dangling as if they had no strength. Harpirias was puzzled at first; but gradually it struck him that what she was doing was imitating Korinaam: his flimsy physique, his way of walking.

Harpirias pointed toward the room that was next to his in the lodge—Korinaam's room. "They are Shapeshifters, you mean?" And he too mimicked Korinaam's manner.

"Yes. Yes. Shapeshifters." Ivla Yevikenik grinned at him and clapped her hands in pleasure at her own success in answering his question.

Shapeshifters! So it was true! Just as he had suspected.

Or had he put the word in her mouth himself? Was she simply telling him what she thought he wanted to hear?

Possibly so. But Harpirias had a hunch that the information she was giving him was accurate. The creatures on the heights, after all, had had the semblance of men while they were dancing; but when they had gone racing off afterward, they had run on all fours in a way that no human being could have managed. The only rational explanation he could find was that they had altered their bodily form to achieve that.

And Korinaam—who had been so evasive when Harpirias twice tried to draw an opinion about them from him—he must have recognized at once that the people of the heights were a band of his own distant kinsmen, some sort of wild Metamorphs of the northland. Which for reasons of his own he had not wanted to confirm.

What would a tribe of wild Shapeshifters be doing by the shores of the Frozen Sea?

Harpirias knew that in the old days before the arrival of the first human settlers, thousands of years ago, the Piurivars had lived wherever they pleased on the giant planet. Their capital city had been at Velalisier in south-central Alhanroel, and its stupendous stone ruins were still there for all to see. There had been other Metamorph settlements, now vanished without a trace, on the other side of the Inner Sea in the forests of Zimroel, and even in the desert wastes of the isolated southern continent of Suvrael. But why would they have gone into the frigid northlands? So far as anyone was aware, Metamorphs were people who preferred warm climates.

Harpirias thought once more of the creation fable that Korinaam had told him during their journey up from Ni-moya—the one about the great beast that had wandered the northern mountains in solitude, the only inhabitant of the world, and had brought the first Piurivars into being by carving them from the ice with her tongue. From that tale Harpirias had learned that the Piurivars believed this chilly northland to be their earliest home, from which they had eventually launched the migrations that would send them radiating outward over all of Majipoor.

Were these wild devils of the ice the last remnant of that archaic Metamorph population, still roaming the broken and tormented landscape of the ancestral territory of their race?

Probably not, Harpirias thought. More likely the myth of a northern origin was only a myth and this was some forgotten group that had fled to the extreme north seeking refuge at the time of the conquest of Majipoor by humans. Who had simply remained in these remote districts ever since, their existence unknown even to their Metamorph kin, just as the Othinor had maintained themselves undisturbed in their secluded mountain-ringed hiding place all these centuries.

"Tell me more," he said to the girl. "Everything you know about them."

There was little enough to tell. Slowly, with all the patience he could muster, he drew what there was of it from her.

"They are the Eililylal," she said. He supposed that that was the Othinor name for them; and Harpirias recalled, an instant later, that that also was the word Toikella had shouted in his rage, the word that Korinaam had translated as "enemies—enemies." Perhaps the word had two meanings in Othinor, the other one being the name of the hated Shapeshifter tribe of the highlands; but Korinaam would not have known that.

Ivla Yevikenik told him that the Eililylal descended periodically out of their barren inhospitable territory to cause trouble for the Othinor, stealing their stored supplies of dried meat and raiding their animal pens. In years gone by there had been a great war between the Othinor and the Eililylal; even now, the Othinor made a practice of killing on sight any Eililylal they happened to encounter.

And now the Eililylal had returned to the Othinor land. They were the ones, said Ivla Yevikenik, who lately had been slaying the sacred hajbaraks and throwing their corpses down into the village as tokens of mockery. No one knew why. Possibly it was the beginning of some new war between the tribes. The king was deeply troubled by it, and his uneasiness had been greatly increased by the appearance of a contingent of Eililylal in the highlands during the royal hunt—a sign of profound bad luck. That was why he had called the hunt off as soon as he had found at least one animal to slay.

More than that, the girl was unable to say.

But she had given him something to start with. Harpirias was grateful for that much, and he told her so, as well as he could manage it. Ivla Yevikenik evidently understood his meaning, and was pleased.

Harpirias realized that he was coming to like Ivla Yevikenik very much, that he was in fact thankful for the circumstances that had forced them together. Not only was she an eager and passionate lover, but she was good-hearted and friendly as well, the lone island of warmth that he had found in this grim land.

Outside, a fierce wind was roaring through the open village square. Harpirias shivered. Just another lovely summer night among the Othinor.

Affectionately he traced the outline of the girl's cheeks with his fingertips, and even let his hand linger a moment over the ornamental sliver of bone in her upper lip. She made a little sighing sound and wriggled up close against him. She licked the tips of his fingers; she nibbled his chin; she caught hold of both his wrists and squeezed them with surprising force.

Strange as it may sound, he imagined himself telling the Coronal one day, *I found it appropriate for reasons of diplomatic necessity to become the lover of King Toikella's daughter. As it turned out, however, the barbarian princess was young and beautiful, and a fiery and uninhibited bedmate besides, well versed in the strange amorous skills of her people—*

Oh, yes. His lordship would certainly love that part of the story.

But there was the little matter of getting out of here and back to Castle Mount first.

13

In the morning, when Ivla Yevikenik had wrapped herself in her furs and left his room, Harpirias went looking for Korinaam. He had a few questions to ask him about their encounter with the Metamorphs of the high country. But Korinaam was nowhere to be found, neither in his room nor anywhere else in the Othinor village.

"When did you last see him?" Harpirias asked Eskenazo Marabaud.

"Last night, around the time they brought our evening meal to the lodging house," the Skandar captain replied.

"Did he say anything to you then?"

"Not a thing, no. Stared at me for an instant in that fishy way of theirs—you know what I mean. And then just walked down the corridor and disappeared into his room."

But the Ghayrog Mizguun Troyzt, who needed no sleep because this was not his season of hibernation, was able to provide better information. During the late hours of the night Mizguun Troyzt had gone out of the village enclosure to the place where they had left the floaters, so that he could oil their rotors against the cold and perform other routine maintenance on them; and, returning in the darkness just before the dawn, he had seen the Shapeshifter crossing the village plaza by himself, heading for the passageway that ran behind the royal palace.

Mizguun Troyzt had watched for a moment or two in idle curiosity as Korinaam circled around toward the far side of the palace and melted into the shadows. Then—it was, after all, no business of his what the Shapeshifter might be up to—Mizguun Troyzt had returned to his own room to await the new day. And that was the last time, apparently, that he or anyone else had seen Korinaam.

What was in back of the royal palace?

Why, the beginning of the trail that led up the mountain wall to the royal hunting preserve.

Of course! Of course! The situation was instantly clear to Harpirias. Korinaam must have gone off to make contact with his newly discovered Shapeshifter brethren in the high country above the village!

Which was perplexing and maddening. The negotiations with King Toikella had not yet really even begun, after all this time. In recent days the king had been far too preoccupied with the advent of the Eililylal in his territory to make himself available for discussions of any sort with Harpirias.

And now here was the official interpreter and guide

blithely vanishing into the high country on an unauthorized errand without so much as a by-your-leave. How long was Korinaam going to be gone? Three days? Five? What if he never returned at all, but fell victim up there to the stark conditions of the trail, or the unpredictable hostility of his own kinsmen?

In that case, how would the treaty with the Othinor ever be worked out, and the hostages set free, without an interpreter? And there was something even more important to consider. How, Harpirias wondered, were he and his soldiers going to find their way back to civilization without the Metamorph's help?

He boiled with rage. There was nothing he could do, though, except wait.

Three days went by; and Harpirias's anger and impatience mounted steadily. The only comforts he found were in the girl Ivla Yevikenik, and in the dark bitter beer of the village. But he could make love only so much, and drink only so much, before even those palliatives ceased to have any effect. Nor were his traveling companions of much benefit to him. They were common soldiers and he was a prince of the Mount, after all, and they were Skandars and Ghayrogs besides. No friendship was possible there. Essentially he was alone in this place.

Fretfully Harpirias roamed the village, desperate for diversion. No one blocked his way; he went wherever he pleased. Or nearly so: evidently he would not be permitted to visit the hostages in their cave, for one morning when he saw the daily trek of food-carriers setting out for them he attempted to join the march, but he was firmly turned aside. Otherwise the Othinor placed no restrictions on his movements. Unchallenged, Harpirias went out to inspect the flat stone altar in the middle of the plaza, and saw that its surface was inscribed with faint incomprehensible glyphs and stained with the dried blood of old sacrifices. He peered into dark musty ice-caverns where foodstuffs were stored, the roots and grains and berries that the inhabitants of this miserable land gathered during the summer foragings against the frightful winter that would soon descend. He opened the leather door of a low dome-shaped ice building he had not noticed before, and found himself facing a room full of small snarling animals tied down with leather harnesses. Entering another, he came upon seven or eight fat-bellied heavy-breasted women of the king's harem, lying naked on thick stacks of furs and smoking long narrow pipes of bone. The air in there was stale and close, reeking with the stench of sweat and some evil perfume and whatever it was that they were smoking. The women giggled shrilly and gestured as though to beckon Harpirias within, but he made a quick exit.

The interior of yet another building where crude wooden boxes were stacked smelled of incense and dust: Harpirias lifted the lid of one box and saw dried human skulls inside, old ones, yellowed and crumbling.

He asked Ivla Yevikenik about that.

"A very holy place," she said. "You must not go in there again."

Whose skulls were they? Those of former kings? Dead priests? Defeated foes? Harpirias realized that he would probably never find out. But what did it matter, anyway? He hadn't come here to carry out an anthropological study of these people, but only to wrest a pack of fatuous fossil-hunters from their grasp—which perhaps he might never accomplish, for another light snowfall had occurred on the third day of Korinaam's absence. Harpirias was convinced now that the Shapeshifter must have perished somewhere in the high country. His body was lying hidden beneath a blanket of snow; in all likelihood it would never be found.

And so it well might be, Harpirias reflected, that he was going to spend the rest of his days in this miserable little icebound village at the far edge of the world, living on charred roots and half-cooked chunks of meat. Was it possible that the skulls in those boxes were those of previous distinguished ambassadors from the outer world, and that his own was destined to rest among them, one of these days?

These endless idle hours seemed interminable. He felt like a prisoner here, like one of those miserable sequestered men in their ice cave high up the canyon wall. At night, lying in the arms of Ivla Yevikenik, he prayed for some reassuring dream. If only the blessed Lady of the Isle, whose spirit roved the world at night bringing welcome balm and surcease to the trou-

14

On the evening of the fourth day since the disappearance of Korinaam, Harpirias was dozing alone in his room when word came that the Shapeshifter had at last returned.

"Bring him to me," he told Eskenazo Marabaud.

Korinaam looked pale and haggard from his adventure. His robe was soiled and torn, his slit-like lips were tightly compressed, his eyelids were swollen, hooding his eyes so that they could hardly be seen at all. He held himself in a tense, edgy way, as though he might be thinking of undergoing transformation into some other guise and making an escape. Harpirias imagined Korinaam turning himself suddenly into a long serpentine ribbon, swiftly gliding out of the room while he sought in vain to catch hold of him.

"Do you want me to stay?" the Skandar asked. Perhaps something along those same lines had occurred to him.

Harpirias nodded. To Korinaam he said coldly, "Where have you been?"

Korinaam was slow to reply.

"On a little reconnaissance mission," he said at length.

"I don't remember asking you to undertake any such mission. Where were you performing this reconnaissance?"

"Around. About."

"Be more specific."

"It was a private matter." There was a note of defiance in the Metamorph's tone.

"I realize that," said Harpirias. "I still want to know the details."

He signaled to Eskenazo Marabaud. "Hold him, will you? I don't want him vanishing on me."

The Skandar, who was standing behind Korinaam, wrapped two of his arms around the Shapeshifter's chest. Korinaam looked amazed. His eyes opened as wide as Harpirias had ever seen them, and he glared at Harpirias in unconcealed hatred.

"Now," Harpirias said coolly. "Once more, Korinaam. Tell me where you went."

The Shapeshifter remained silent for a time. Then he said, reluctantly, "To the heights overlooking the village."

"Yes. I rather thought so. And just why did you go there?"

Korinaam seemed ready to burst with indignation. "Prince, I demand that you order your Skandar to let go of me! You have no right—"

Harpirias cut him off. "I have every right. You happen to be here in the employment of the Coronal and you've chosen to go off on an unauthorized side journey at a time when your services were needed. I want an explanation. Again: what were you looking for up there, Korinaam?"

"I refuse to discuss my private affairs with you."

"You have no private affairs in this place. —Twist his arm a little, Eskenazo Marabaud."

"This is an absolute outrage!" Korinaam cried. "I am a free citizen of—"

"Yes. Of course you are. No one denies that. —Twist it a little harder, will you, Eskenazo Marabaud? Until he yelps a little. Or until he gives me the answers I want. Don't worry, it won't break. You can't break a Shapeshifter's arm, you know. The bones simply give with the stress, like rubber. But you can hurt him, all the same. It will be quite all right to hurt him if he doesn't cooperate. Yes, that's the way. —What were you looking for up there, Korinaam?"

Silence. Harpirias looked toward the Skandar and made a twisting gesture with his hands.

"I was looking for the people we saw on the ridge the day of the hunt," Korinaam said sullenly.

"Ah. I'm not surprised to hear that. And why did you want to find them?"

Silence.

"Twist," Harpirias told the Skandar.

Korinaam said, "Are you aware that this is interrogation under torture? It's barbaric! It's unthinkable!"

"You have my sincerest apologies," said Harpirias. "Will your arm break after all, I wonder, if he twists it far enough? We don't really want to find out, do we, Korinaam? Tell me: Who were those people we saw on the ridge?"

"That's what I was trying to find out."

"No. You already know who they are, don't you? Tell me. Tell me, Korinaam. *Who are they?*"

"Piurivars," Korinaam murmured, looking down toward the ground.

"Are they, now? Cousins of yours?"

"So to speak. Distant cousins. Very distant."

Harpirias nodded. "Thank you. —You can let go of him, Eskenazo Marabaud. He seems to be more cooperative now. Wait outside, will you?" To the Metamorph he said, once the Skandar had gone, "All right. Tell me what you know about these distant cousins, Korinaam."

But Korinaam claimed to know very little about them, and Harpirias had the feeling that for once he was sincere.

There were, Korinaam said, old legends among his people to the effect that one branch of the Metamorph race had settled in the far north in the time of Lord Stiamot, many thousands of years ago—Piurivars who had escaped, as Harpirias had already guessed, from the genocidal war that Lord Stiamot had launched against the aboriginal inhabitants of the planet.

While all the rest of the surviving Metamorphs had been rounded up and confined in the reservation set aside for them in the jungles of Zimroel—so the tale went—these free Piurivars had continued to dwell in isolation and independence, following the ancient nomadic ways of their people in the snowy and mountainous country beyond the nine great peaks of the Khyntor Marches. Like the Othinor, they had lived as a people apart, unknown to the other inhabitants of Majipoor and perhaps, after all this time, equally unaware of them. There had never been any communication between them and other Metamorphs, not even during Valentine's reign, when the great Piurivar uprising against human rule had taken place. Their very existence had become a matter of conjecture and speculation.

Now and again a sighting was reported by one of the Shapeshifters who, like Korinaam, lived in Ni-moya or some other city bordering on the Marches and made their livings providing guide service to hunters or explorers that wished to venture into the north country. But none of those sightings had ever led to anything. It was impossible for the Metamorph guides even to be sure that what they were seeing—always at a great distance, for just a fleeting moment—were people of their own kind.

Until now.

"I have no doubt of it," Korinaam said. "My eyesight is very keen, prince. The day we saw them, I watched them undergo their change."

"And so you decided to take off without authorization to visit them. Why?"

"They are of my blood, prince. For nearly nine thousand years now they have lived in these mountains without ever once coming face-to-face with others of their kind. I wanted to speak with them."

"And tell them what?"

"That the persecution is over, that we Piurivars are free to come and go as we please on Majipoor, that they can emerge at last from their hiding place amidst the snow and ice. Is that so difficult for you to understand, prince?"

"You could have told me what you intended to do, at least. You could have asked my permission."

"You would never have given it."

Harpirias was caught off guard by that. His face reddened. "Why do you say so?"

"Because," said Korinaam evenly, "I am a Piurivar, and this is a Piurivar affair, and why would any of that matter in the slightest to you, prince? You would have said that it was inconvenient for me to leave the village, because I was needed here as your interpreter. You would have told me that I could return to these mountains at another time, on my own, and look for my kinsmen then. Is that not so, prince?"

Suddenly Harpirias had difficulty meeting the Shapeshifter's implacable gaze. He could make no immediate reply.

"Possibly it is," he said finally. "But even so: you still shouldn't have gone off without leaving some sort of message about where you were going. What would we have done if you had died up there?"

"I had no intention of dying up there."

"It's a difficult climb in dangerous territory. There was a snowstorm during the time you were gone. A light one, but suppose it had been one like the one we rode through in the pass of the Twin Sisters? You aren't immortal, Korinaam."

"I know how to take care of myself in these mountains. As you see, I have returned, and only slightly the worse for wear."

"Yes. So you have."

Korinaam offered no response. He continued to stare at Harpirias with undisguised animosity.

This was all becoming very uncomfortable. Somehow Korinaam had gained the upper hand in the discussion, though Harpirias was not quite sure when that had happened. It embarrassed him deeply now that he had felt compelled to resort to arm-twisting in order to make the Shapeshifter speak.

He said, after an awkward pause, "Well? And did you succeed in having a talk with these long-lost relatives of yours, then?"

"Not exactly."

"What does that mean?"

"I talked *to* them," said Korinaam. "Not *with* them."

"Ah. To them but not with them. Meaning that you couldn't speak to them in a language they understood?"

Korinaam said, in a tense and ragged tone, "That is essentially what happened. —Do we really need to discuss this any further, prince?"

"Yes. We do. I want to know precisely what took place between you and those people."

"I've told you. For two days I searched for them, and then I found them, camped on a hillside across a ravine opposite the place where I was. It was impossible for me to get really close, but I tried to speak with them from where I stood; they didn't seem to comprehend anything I was saying; after a little while I gave up and headed back down the mountain."

"That's all?

"All, yes."

"Your shape is flickering around the edges, Korinaam. You can't hold yourself still, do you know that? What that says to me is that you're lying."

Hoarsely the Metamorph replied, "I found them and I was unable to communicate with them in any useful way, and then I left and came back here. That's the whole story."

"I don't think it is," said Harpirias. "What else happened up there?"

"Nothing. Nothing." A ripple of change passed swiftly across Korinaam's features, betraying inner turmoil. He was hiding something, something that had shaken him deeply during his meeting with his wild kinsmen of the high country. Harpirias had no doubt of that.

"Do you want me to get the Skandar back in here for a little more arm-twisting?"

Korinaam glared malevolently. "All right. There was something else."

"Go on."

"They threw rocks at me," he said in a bitter, husky tone.

"I can't say I'm surprised."

"I explained to them who I was. When I saw that they didn't understand my words I showed them that I was one of them by doing changes for them, prince. And they threw—rocks at me."

That moment of hesitation in Korinaam's voice aroused Harpirias's interest.

"That's all they did? Throw rocks?"

More flickerings, more ripplings.

"Tell me, Korinaam. I need to know what sort of creatures we're dealing with."

The Shapeshifter trembled. Words burst from him in an angry rush. "They spat at me also. And then they threw their—their dung at me. They picked it up in their hands and hurled it across the ravine. And while they did it they danced about and screamed at me like crazy people. Like devils." There was a terrible expression on his face. "They are loathsome things. They are worse than savages! They are *animals.*"

"I see."

"And now you have heard it all. Will you let me alone now, prince?"

"In a moment," said Harpirias. "First tell me this: will you make another attempt to communicate with them?"

"You can be certain that I have no intention of that."

"And why is that?"

"Are you a fool, prince? Can't you understand simple words? What I saw up there was utterly disgusting. It was hideous to be near them—to watch them capering like beasts—to listen to their revolting screeches—to think that they were actually—of Piurivar blood—that they and I—"

Softly Harpirias said, "I understand all that, Korinaam. But even so: if I were to ask you to make another journey to see them, would you do it?"

Korinaam was silent for a time.

"If you ordered me to, yes."

"Only if I made it an order?"

"I have no desire to see those creatures again, none at all. But I am aware that I am in the service of the Coronal, whose representative you are, and it is not possible for me to defy your direct order, prince. You may rest assured of that." The Shapeshifter bowed deeply, giving Harpirias a harshly exaggerated salute of deference. "I am not eager to have my arm twisted a second time."

"I regret that it was necessary to do that, Korinaam."

"I'm sure that you do. It must have been extremely disagreeable for you. And quite distasteful for the Skandar too, I would think."

"I told you I regretted it. By the Divine, Korinaam, do you want me to get down and beg your forgiveness? You were being infuriatingly evasive. And insubordinate to boot. I needed to know where you had gone, and why." Harpirias made an impatient dismissive gesture. "Enough of this. Go, now. But in the future you're not to take a step anywhere outside of this village without permission. Is that clear?"

"Where would I want to go?" asked the Shapeshifter, rubbing his arm.

When he had gone, Harpirias called Eskenazo Marabaud back into the room and instructed him to keep watch on Korinaam's movements.

"The young woman is here," the Skandar told him. "The one who comes to you at night."

Was that a note of disapproval in his voice? From a Skandar?

"Send her in," Harpirias said.

15

In the middle of the night he was awakened from deep and happy slumber by muffled thumps, angry shouts, and then the sound of a long agonized wailing scream. It took him a moment, or perhaps more than that, to realize that he was not dreaming. As he struggled up toward full wakefulness another scream came, and another, and Harpirias recognized the voice of the screamer as that of Korinaam, calling out for help.

He scrambled out from under the pile of hides. Ivla Yevikenik clutched sleepily at him, trying to draw him back, but Harpirias shook her off. Hastily dressing, he rushed into the corridor. A blast of glacial air struck him there: the main entrance to the building stood ajar. He looked into Korinaam's room. Empty. There were signs of a struggle. Harpirias could hear Korinaam still howling, his shrill cries a mixture of rage and panic. Quickly he ran outside.

A strange scene was being enacted in front of the lodge.

Two burly Othinor warriors were dragging the writhing,

screaming, kicking Korinaam toward the stone altar, where King Toikella, the high priest, and some of the other important men of the tribe waited in a grim little circle. The king, clad from head to toe in a bulky swaddling of black haigus furs, gripped with both his hands the hilt of an enormous sword that stood before him, its tip thrust into the icy ground.

Eight or ten of the Skandars were in the plaza also. They must have emerged from the lodge in response to Korinaam's cries for help, and were following uncertainly along behind the Shapeshifter now. They held their energy-throwers at ready, but obviously they were unwilling to take action without a direct order from Harpirias.

Harpirias caught up with them and asked Eskenazo Marabaud what was happening.

"They are going to kill him, prince."

"What? Why?"

But the Skandar only shrugged.

Indeed Korinaam had arrived at the altar now and his Othinor captors had flung him down upon it. He lay spread-eagled, quivering in fear, his body flickering through a host of apparently random form-changes with unsettling rapidity, entering some bizarre bestial shape for a moment, then becoming disturbingly human, then reverting to the Metamorph form, but terribly contorted and almost unrecognizable. Several of the Othinor, kneeling beside the stone slab, held him tight. Plainly they were startled by the strange flurry of changes, but they gripped him valiantly all the same. A couple of them seemed to be fastening ropes around Korinaam's limbs and tying them to pegs that were set in the ground alongside the altar's perimeter.

Cursing, Harpirias went sprinting forward. The king, somber and immense in his thick black furs, held up a hand to halt him when he was still fifteen or twenty paces from the altar. Solemnly Toikella pointed to the great sword, pointed to Korinaam, made a graphic gesture of execution.

"No!" Harpirias bellowed. "I forbid it!" He stamped his foot and gesticulated ferociously with outspread arms. Toikella might not understand his words, but he would certainly comprehend the displeasure that his urgent tone of voice and violent movements conveyed.

The king scowled, shook his head, pulled the sword from the ground, and slowly began to swing it aloft.

Harpirias responded with even more frantic gestures and a desperate babble of words in what he hoped was comprehensible Othinor—fragments of half-understood phrases that he had learned from Ivla Yevikenik, a torrential stream of blurted exclamations which might or might not make sense, but which perhaps would at least give King Toikella a moment's pause.

His garbled outcry seemed to have the desired effect. The king, with a puzzled growl, halted in mid-swing and thrust the sword back into the ground, rocking forward and pressing his weight on it, all the while staring at Harpirias as though he had gone out of his mind.

Harpirias approached the altar. Toikella remained utterly still. To the mystified king Harpirias signaled in furious pantomime that the cords binding Korinaam must be removed. The king made no response, but merely continued to lean on the great sword and glower. Out of the corner of his eye Harpirias saw other Othinor warriors, brandishing spears and swords, quietly heading across the plaza toward the altar.

Some of the Skandars had come up behind Harpirias now also. He beckoned them in even closer to him. "Spread out in a semicircle in back of me," he told them. "Draw and arm your energy-throwers. But be very careful not to point them in the direction of the king. And no matter what happens, don't fire unless I say so."

He looked down at Korinaam, supine and trembling on the altar.

"All right. What in the name of the Divine has been going on here?"

Korinaam's slitlike lips moved, but no coherent speech came out. His eyes were glazed.

"Speak, man! Tell me!"

With intense effort the Shapeshifter said in a faint quavering voice, "They thought—spying—enemies—"

"Enemies? The high-country Shapeshifters, you mean. Their name means 'enemies' here. *Eililylal.*"

From Toikella, at that recognizable word, came a grunt of perceptible surprise.

"Speak to me," Harpirias said to Korinaam. "The king thought you were a spy for the wild Shapeshifters up there, is that it?"

Feebly Korinaam nodded.

"And was going to sacrifice you on the altar?"

Another nod.

"I ought to let him do it!"

"You know I am no spy." Korinaam could barely get the words out. "Please. Please, prince. Tell him that."

"You want *me* to tell him?"

"I am—too frightened—" The merest whisper.

"Too frightened to beg him for your own life?"

"Please—please—" The Metamorph on the altar quivered and shook.

Scared out of his wits. Harpirias snorted in frustration. The king was looking restless. Already he seemed to be on the verge of pulling the great sword from the ground once again.

It was time to invoke a higher authority.

"Coronal!" Harpirias cried, waving his arms about importantly. "Cor-o-*nal.*" King Toikella frowned. "Coronal," Harpirias said again, putting a snap of command into his tone. He pointed to the sky. "Lord Ambinole. Coronal of Majipoor."

He groped for words. But his Othinor had deserted him in the confusion of the moment. Conversing with Ivla Yevikenik in the privacy of his room was much easier for him. Suddenly, what little Harpirias had learned of the grammar was mostly rubble and half the vocabulary was gone from his mind. But he had to speak. He remembered the Othinor word that he thought meant "lordship," and offered that: *"Helminthak."* The word seemed to have an effect of some sort on the king. Then Harpirias pointed at Toikella and shook his head emphatically. Lamely he said in Majipoori, "You must not kill him. Coronal say, must not kill. Must—not—kill. Servant of Coronal!"

Toikella appeared baffled. But he allowed the sword's tip to remain embedded in the ground.

"Cor-o-nal," said Harpirias once more, enunciating slowly and carefully, as though the word were a powerful talisman. "Coronal of Majipoor. *Helminthak.*" He pantomimed the undoing of Korinaam's bonds and the rising of the Shapeshifter from the altar. Toikella stared at him. And stared. And stared. His eyes grew wider and wider. A low rumbling sound came from him.

He certainly must believe I've gone crazy, Harpirias thought.

Then he realized that the king was staring not at him but at someone or something behind him. Was that quietly encroaching band of tribal warriors about to break into all-out attack? Were the Skandars up to something?

Harpirias glanced quickly back over his shoulder.

Ivla Yevikenik stood there. In the frosty midnight air she

wore only a short cloak of loosely stitched hides casually thrown over bare skin. Fear and uncertainty were visible on her face. She was the only woman of the tribe out here by the altar, and plainly she had no business being here. The look of astonishment and barely suppressed rage on her father's face seemed to confirm that. But when she looked toward Harpirias her eyes began to shine with unmistakable love.

She sees that there is trouble and she has come out here to offer me her assistance, he told himself. At great risk to herself. That must be it. Must be.

In one swift movement Harpirias reached for the girl, caught her gently but firmly by one wrist, and drew her to his side. He folded his arm close around her so that he and she would confront the king as a single entity. Her warmth against his body was welcome in this stinging night chill.

Speaking hesitantly, doing the best he could with his lame and barely comprehensible Othinor supplemented with much pointing and miming, Harpirias told her that he was indeed in need of her help, that Korinaam must be spared from Toikella's anger.

Did she understand? It was galling not to be able to communicate clearly in words with these people. But a little of his meaning appeared to have registered on her, at least. She spoke at some length to her father, who scowled and growled as he listened, but he heard her out, however reluctantly. When she was done he replied with no more than a few curt syllables. She spoke again; and again the king replied, more elaborately this time. He signaled to one of his men. The ropes tying Korinaam to the altar were loosened.

Haltingly Ivla Yevikenik explained to Harpirias what he already knew in essence: that the Othinor had observed Korinaam's recent comings and goings in the high country, and they believed that it was his intention somehow to betray the village to his kinsmen of the mountains. As a suspected ally of the Eililylal, therefore, Korinaam's life was forfeit to the Othinor. Only as a courtesy to the great Coronal Lord of Majipoor had the Shapeshifter been spared, she said. But if Korinaam made any further attempts to contact the Elilylal he would die regardless.

"No," Harpirias said. "He is not the ally of the Eililylal. He is the enemy of the Eililylal. Tell the king that."

She gave him a questioning frown. He said it all again, slowly and with gestures. There was another long colloquy between Ivla Yevikenik and the king, too low and fast for Harpirias to catch the sense of it. He heard the word "Eililylal" repeated many times. At one point the king seized the hilt of his sword and shook it furiously.

To Korinaam Harpirias said, "I could slit your throat myself. Look at the mess you've caused! Tell me what they're saying now, will you? Are they going to kill you or not?"

The Shapeshifter, who had arisen and stood shivering nearby, seemed to have recovered somewhat from his terror.

"The king will permit me to live," he said in a tentative, shaky voice. "But I am to be expelled from the village at once."

"What? What? By the Divine—"

"You yourself are permitted to remain," Korinaam said. "The treaty negotiations will continue."

"Without an interpreter? And who's going to lead us back to Ni-moya when this is over? Oh, no, no, Korinaam, we aren't going to let you be expelled!" An idea was beginning to spring to life in Harpirias's mind. He released his grip on Ivla Yevikenik and reached for the Metamorph instead, catching him by the loose fabric at his throat. "What's going to happen instead is that you're going to go up into those mountains and find the Eililylal, and you're going to order them to clear out of the neighborhood. And you'll make it stick with whatever spooky Shapeshifter magic you're able to command."

Korinaam looked horror-stricken.

"What are you saying? Magic? I am no magician, prince! I am simply one who guides visitors that wish to see the north country. Find yourself some little Vroon, if wizardry is what you want. And as for ordering those people to do anything—how could I possibly do that?"

"You'll do it, all right, and that's all there is to it." Harpirias let go of Korinaam's garment and shoved him a few paces away. To Ivla Yevikenik he said, "Tell your father that we offer our services in ridding his land of the Eililylal. Do you follow me? Eililylal—*out.* We will do! Korinaam and I, with my soldiers! Yes? No more Eililylal. By my solemn oath. But the assistance of Korinaam is needed. Needed very much. Tell him that!"

The girl smiled, turned to her father, began to speak.

"Prince, what are you promising them?" Korinaam asked. His face was a study in anguish and despair.

"What I have in mind is this," said Harpirias. "I'm going to tell you and then, if you think you have your wits about you again, you'll explain it to the king for me. I want you to stand on your hind legs in front of him and let him know that you are a mighty sorcerer and that on his behalf you will devote all of your energies and powers to driving off the wild Shapeshifters of the mountains, whom you loathe and despise. Is that clear? Tell him that the army of the Lord Coronal of Majipoor, led in person by me, will go back up into the high country in the morning and make a maximum show of force to impress the Eililylal while you are casting your spells; and in return for all this, once the Eililylal have been duly driven off, the king will free the hostages and we will take our leave of his village and everyone will live happily ever after. Tell him that, Korinaam."

"Prince—this matter of casting spells—"

"Tell him what I want you to tell him," Harpirias said ominously. "Every word, just as I spoke it. Ivla Yevikenik will be listening, and she'll report to me on the accuracy of your translation. Nothing will help you if you try to trick me, Korinaam. I'll let the king know that it's fine with me if he wants to put you back on that altar and slit your throat, and I'll help tie you down myself. Is that understood, Korinaam? Is it?"

"Yes, prince. It is."

"Good. Start talking, then."

16

Finding the Eililylal, of course, was easier promised than accomplished. It took three days, three disagreeable days of marching hither and thither in the heights, while the north wind blew almost unceasingly and occasional sprinklings of light snow fell to remind Harpirias that the short Othinor summer was almost at its end.

More than once his plan began to seem like a fool's errand to him. A huge expeditionary force had gone up into the mountains: not only Korinaam and Harpirias and the entire military force of Skandars and Ghayrogs, but also King Toikella and the high priest Mankhelm and some thirty or forty warriors of the tribe. For this sparsely populated part of the world, that was an enormous army. Surely the Eililylal, watching such a horde make its way up the canyon trails from the village to the high country, would prudently take to their heels and scurry back to their own territory in the deep north until it seemed safe to venture into the vicinity of the Othinor again.

But Harpirias was reckoning on two factors that he hoped would work in his favor. One was the mischief that the wild Shapeshifters had been up to among the king's hajbaraks. He suspected that the killing of the first two, and the hurling of them into the Othinor village, had been only the prelude to some more elaborate hostile event that they were contemplating. Since that had not happened yet, they were probably still somewhere in the neighborhood.

The other factor was sheer Eililylal malevolence: their obvious love of making trouble, their eagerness to do things like slaughtering the king's sacred beasts and tossing them down into the village, or of dancing and capering obscenely on a high ridge when the king came up from the village to look for them, or the reception that they had provided for Korinaam. This bigger force, with its multitude of armed Othinor warriors and its array of great lumbering Skandars, might just tempt them to come forth again for an even livelier display of mockery than before.

Which indeed proved to be the case.

They appeared, finally, just when Harpirias had almost given up hope of finding them and King Toikella was beginning to study Korinaam in a sinisterly appraising sort of way. It was Mankhelm who saw them first. The gaunt high priest had gone off the trail by himself to perform some morning ritual on an outcropping ledge looking into a shallow side canyon; and suddenly he came rushing back all helter-skelter, trailing his holy ribbons and pouches of sacred powders casually from one hand, signaling wildly with the other, and crying loudly, "Eililylal! Eililylal!"

They were arrayed along the upper crags of the opposite face of the little side canyon: a band of scrawny ragged-looking creatures, twenty, thirty, perhaps even fifty of them, perching on the rocks and quietly staring down at the army of the Othinor.

The distance across to them was not great; it seemed possible almost to reach across and touch them. In the bright morning sunlight it was beyond question that they were Metamorphs. They had the long frail attenuated bodies, the minimal facial features, the pale green skins. They seemed to have set up a camp over there, with five or six crude tents of roughly dressed animal skins. Tools and what looked like simple weapons lay scattered around in front of them—spears, and bows and arrows, and, perhaps, blow-darts. Savages like the Othinor is what they are, thought Harpirias. Brutish primitive folk who lived dark and difficult lives in this pitiless land.

They had two of Toikella's hajbaraks with them. The big thick-furred quadrupeds lay on their sides with their hocks tethered together and gazed sadly into space. Very likely, Harpirias suspected, the Eililylal had been making ready to do some harm to the sacrosanct beasts for Toikella's greater displeasure, but had halted when Mankhelm had come upon them.

Harpirias glanced toward Korinaam and said, "Tell the king to send half his warriors around to the right and half to the left. It should be possible to get over to the other rim of this canyon not very far from here. They should take up positions flanking the Eililylal on either side and wait there for orders."

While Korinaam was relaying these instructions, Harpirias moved his own forces forward onto the ledge facing the Metamorphs, arraying them in a long line against the breast of the mountain with their energy-throwers armed and ready.

"Now," Harpirias told the Shapeshifter, "you go out to the edge of the outcropping and call across to your friends over there. Tell them in your own language that they are ordered in the name of all the gods of the Piurivars to depart from the territory of the Othinor at once."

"They won't understand a word I'm saying."

"Very likely that's so. Do it anyway. Tell them that the gods in their holy wisdom have assigned this territory to the Unchanging Ones, or whatever it is that you people call us, and that all Piurivars have to leave here right away."

"We do not exactly have gods in the sense that you—"

"You have *something* that you regard as divine. Invoke it."

Korinaam sighed. "As you wish, prince."

"I should tell you, also, in case you're unaware of it, that Eskenazo Marabaud is fluent in the Piurivar language." So far as Harpirias knew, that was untrue; but he doubted that Korinaam would call his bluff. "If he should notify me that you've said anything treacherous instead of what I've asked you to say, Korinaam, I'll push you off that ledge with my own hands."

Icily the Shapeshifter said, "What treachery would be possible? I've told you already that those creatures over there are unfamiliar with any civilized language."

"You've told me that, yes. But can I be sure that it's true?"

Anger flared in Korinaam's eyes. "I am here to do your bidding, prince, and nothing but your bidding. You may count on that."

"Good. Thank you. Now: after you've made your little speech about the will of the Piurivar gods, you're going to start casting spells. You'll make them up as you go along: I know you're good at that. Cry out any sort of crazy mumbo-jumbo that comes to your mind. Just do it in an appropriately awesome incantatory tone. And while you're doing it, I want you to screech and howl and dance around exactly as we saw the Eililylal doing the last time we were up here. But with five times as much frenzy and noise."

Korinaam gasped in astonishment. "Surely this is not a serious request!"

"You'd be wise to treat it as one."

"Then you are asking a great deal of me. This is a clown's work, prince. Do you take me for a performer? Someone from the Perpetual Circus of Dulorn, perhaps?"

"You don't need to be a stage actor in order to screech and

howl, Korinaam. Just give it everything you've got, nothing held back, some nice wild shrieking and leaping around. Do you follow me? I want you to scare them. I want you to scare *yourself.* Give us the kind of act that would get somebody locked up if he did it on the streets of Ni-moya, do you understand? This is no time for being shy, Korinaam. Really put your heart in it. Or whatever it is you may have that passes for a heart."

"But this is humiliating, prince! What you ask me to do goes against my temperament, my character, the very integrity of my being!"

"I take formal note of your objections," said Harpirias calmly. "I remind you that there's an altar waiting for you down in the village if you prefer not to cooperate."

Korinaam glared, but made no reply.

"And while you're casting your spells," Harpirias went on, "you will also be making a series of highly dramatic changes."

"Changes?"

"Changes, yes. Bodily metamorphoses. Shifting of shape. Piurivars are known to have that capability, I believe. You will do changes. Your entire repertoire, and possibly some that you have never done before. The stranger the better, do you know what I mean? I want you to make yourself into six kinds of monster. I want you to look demonic and horrifying. I want you to show those cousins of yours over there that you are an absolute master of sorcery and witchcraft and that if they don't obey you you will bring down all the forces of darkness upon their heads. It will be your job to make yourself look just as frightening as anybody has ever looked upon this entire planet. A diabolical ogre. A thing out of everybody's worst nightmares."

The Shapeshifter's eyes were bright with fury.

"What you require of me, prince, is—"

"Is simply to do as you are told."

"I repeat: I am not a clown. I am not an actor. Nor am I a savage, prince. To stand out there and howl and shriek idiotically, and above all to put myself through changes like that, in front of everyone, not just them but your own men, and the king of the Othinor as well, would shame me forever."

"Go, Korinaam. Time is wasting."

"Prince, I ask you—I beg you—"

"The altar, Korinaam. Remember the altar. Go on. Quickly, now. There's no shame in doing one's duty. Your role will be essential today. Perform for us. Give us the best show that's in you. You said that these people were like beasts. Well, give them some of the same stuff, only more so. Behave like a wild man. Out-beast them ten for one. Perform as though your life depends on it. It does, you know."

Korinaam offered no answer; but he shot Harpirias such a look of unalloyed abhorrence as could have thawed a glacier. Harpirias responded with a sweet smile and nudged the Shapeshifter gently toward the front of the outcropping.

The jutting shelf of stone on which Korinaam stood was almost like a little stage. The Eililylal across the way seemed to stir in curiosity as the glowering Metamorph took up his position on it.

He was silent for a time, breathing deeply, staring at the ground. Then he raised his head and extended his arms to their full spread. He flicked his fingers outward two or three times, and made a small humming sound that could barely be heard even on this side of the canyon.

"Louder, Korinaam," Harpirias said. "Wilder. Start putting yourself through some changes."

"Prince, this is ridiculous!"

"The altar, Korinaam. The altar."

The Shapeshifter nodded. He stretched out his arms again. Abruptly the boundaries of his shape wavered and his arms became long ropy tentacles that seemed to writhe of their own accord in agonized serpentine patterns. The Eililylal stirred and exchanged glances with one another.

"Very good," Harpirias said. "Now chant a spell."

"Yes. Give me a moment, will you?"

Korinaam's body continued to change. His shoulders expanded and violently contracted; his skin grew puckered and spiny; his legs turned to hairy wheels; his arms, rigid again, became clubs, spears, long hooked rods.

"Dekkeret!" he cried suddenly. *"Tyeveras Kinniken Malibor Thraym!"*

Harpirias smiled. So the Shapeshifter knew some history after all! Those were the names of Coronals and Pontifexes of long ago, and Korinaam was making an incantation out of them!

"Good," Harpirias murmured. "Keep it up. Faster! Wilder!"

But there was little need for such encouragement. Korinaam seemed to have put all inhibition aside and was getting fully into things now. His form was going through such grotesque alterations as Harpirias could scarcely believe—drawing out to enormous length, then pulling sharply inward like a snapping piece of elastic until he was no more than a huddled cube, and then shooting out a hundred bright pink extensions at once that jerked and quivered with lunatic intensity. Bright blue eyes gleamed at the tip of each rubbery shaft of flesh. Whorls and loops of extruded plasm emerged from him. And all the while he continued to call off the names of ancient monarchs, now crooning them, now droning, now singing in an eerie high-pitched tone that slid between the conventional intervals of the scale with sinuous liberties that would drive any musician to immediate tears:

"Voriax! Valentine! Segilot! Guadeloom, Struin, Arioc! Grivvis! Histifoin! Prankipin, Hunzimar, Spurifon, Scaul!" Then, hissing the name in a truly terrifying way: *"Stiamot. Stiamot. Stiamot."* He accompanied the name of the conqueror of his race with a series of explosive body-shifts that jerked him about the out-

cropping in such a hectic manner that Harpirias feared for a moment that he would go over the side.

Evidently Korinaam had exhausted his memory of the names of Coronals now. He began to chant cities and places instead, while dancing back and forth in high frenzy:

"Bimbak, Dundilmir, Furible, Chi! Dulorn! Ni-moya! Falkynkip! Divone! Ilirivoyne, Kiridane, Mazadone, Nissimorn! Numinor! Pidruid! Piliplok! Gren!"

It was a brilliant performance. Even Harpirias was unsettled a little by the terrible intensity of Korinaam's percussive outcries and seemingly endless metamorphoses. He could almost believe that these *were* genuine spells that were being cast here, that the Shapeshifter was working authentic Piurivar magic in the chill mountain air of this place.

As for the Eililylal across the way, they were mesmerized by it. Perhaps they thought that Korinaam had taken leave of his senses, or perhaps they were taking his spellcasting seriously—who could say? They sat rigidly, watching, watching, watching.

But Harpirias knew that the show could not go on much longer. Surely the metamorphic capacities of any Piurivar's body were unable to keep up such a pace of changes; nor could Korinaam, however durable his slender body might be, continue to prance and cavort and shriek the way he was doing without totally expending his strength.

This was the time for the next phase. Harpirias signaled to

his troops to prepare to open fire. They hefted their weapons and waited for the next command.

To Korinaam, then, he said, "All right. Bring it to a climax. Everything you have. Everything, Korinaam!"

"Danipiur!" Korinaam roared. *"Pontifex! Coronal! Toikella! Majipoor!"*

He rippled and flowed and passed through the entire spectrum of colors, and went through a whole new tumultuous series of bodily changes, now taking on animal forms, now imitating rocks or trees, now presenting himself as pure geometry, now becoming an incomprehensible cluster of tentacles and clacking claws, and then emerging ultimately from the whole blinding welter of astonishing metamorphoses wearing the semblance of King Toikella himself. But it was a Toikella far larger than life, a titanic Toikella, a mountainous Toikella a dozen feet high, identical down to the last degree with the genuine article, except in its size. It was a startling sight. The real Toikella, who had been standing to one side watching throughout the entire performance, now whirled, stared, grunted in amazement. Harpirias saw actual fear blossom in the king's eyes just then.

"Fire!" Harpirias cried.

Three loud cracking reports echoed through the thin, cold mountain air, and then three more, and another, and another. Bolts of purple energy lanced across the canyon, striking high up in the ice-tipped crags far above the ledge where the little band of Eililylal stood watching. Chunks of tawny stone the size of sea-dragons broke loose overhead and tumbled down with ear-shattering impact. They split apart spectacularly as they hit and sent huge showers of fist-sized particles cascading into the depths of the canyon. A low moan of terror went up from the Eililylal.

"Again," Harpirias said. "Aim a little lower."

A second volley of energy bolts crossed the canyon. The purple shafts of force smashed into the rocky walls just below the scars of the first round and carved great sheets of stone from them. Another deafening rain of slabs and boulders descended. Harpirias felt the vibration through the soles of his feet: it was like an earthquake. The entire mountain range seemed to quiver. He thought the world might break asunder.

"All right," he said. "Hold it."

Gradually the sound of the second rockfall died away. A few last pebbles clattered into the chasm, faintly resounding as they fell, and then all was still. Supreme silence followed: the terrible silence of the morning of the world's creation. Through the clear crisp air drifted little sun-gilded puffs of rock dust. Across the way, the Eililylal stood stunned, petrified, frozen by terror into statues.

In that awful moment of utter quiet Harpirias turned to Korinaam and said, "What I want you to do now is tell the king that he needs to—"

But then he saw that finishing the sentence was useless.

Exhausted by his immense effort, emptied entirely of strength, the Shapeshifter—once again in his proper form—had collapsed into a huddled heap, his arms drawn tight against his sunken chest, his entire body shaking in what seemed to be the final extremity of fatigue. Harpirias knew that there was no more service to be had from him just now.

He looked toward the king himself. But once again he was unable to find the Othinor phrases he needed. "Your warriors," he said, urgently pantomiming a band of men with spears. "Send them now. Against the Eililylal. Now! Now!" He acted out the motions of an attack and a massacre.

Toikella merely stared at him. The king, of course, had no way of understanding the Majipoori words that Harpirias had spoken; but that was not the problem. Toikella appeared to be as paralyzed by astonishment and fear as his enemies across the canyon. He looked as though he had been clubbed. His jaw hung slack, his eyes were glassy. There could be no question that Korinaam's bizarre performance had had a deep effect on him, especially at its climax; but plainly it was the destruction that Harpirias's squadron of energy-throwers had meted out that had stupefied him. Nothing in Toikella's experience had prepared himself for the sight of modern Majipoor weaponry in action.

Mankhelm was in no better shape. He was on his knees, looking dazed, fumbling with the holy bones and amulets that dangled on a leather cord around his neck.

Nor in any case was there an Othinor army on the far side of the canyon to mop up the Eililylal, Harpirias realized. The warriors whom Toikella had sent over there to await the order to attack now were coming slinking back in twos and threes, white-faced, shaken. Harpirias threw up his hands in exasperation. "No!" he shouted. "Go across again! Across! Across! Over there! By the Lady, go after the Eililylal now, while you have the chance!"

Mute, bewildered, understanding nothing, they simply gaped at him.

Then Harpirias looked across the way, and with one glance he knew that no attack would be necessary. The Eililylal were gone. They had broken from their terrified stasis and fled pell-mell over the rocky mountain trails, leaving behind their packs, their tents, their weapons and tools, everything they had brought with them from their home encampment somewhere in the farthest north. The two tethered hajbaraks still lay where they had been, unharmed.

It would be an extremely long time, Harpirias suspected, before the wild Metamorphs of the mountains returned to trouble King Toikella's people again.

He walked over to Korinaam and rested his hand lightly on the Shapeshifter's thin shoulder.

"You did very well," Harpirias said quietly. "You were magnificent. Perfect. If the mountain-guide business ever falls off, you could set up shop as a sorcerer and make a fortune."

Korinaam only shrugged.

"Are you very tired?" Harpirias asked.

"What do you think?" His voice carried a freight of anger and embarrassment and, above all else, a deadly, numbing weariness.

"Rest, then. Rest as long as you like. But first tell the king that I've done what I promised. That his enemies have run away, that the war is over. It's safe for him to send his men across the canyon to set free those hajbaraks."

17

When the details of the treaty had been worked out at last, one of Harpirias's Ghayrog soldiers, who fancied himself something of a calligrapher, inscribed its text in duplicate on broad scrolls of bleached leather that Ivla Yevikenik had provided. It was very fine leather, almost of the quality of parchment. Although the treaty was in fact extremely concise, a mere six clauses, the job of lettering it out took three full days, much to Harpirias's annoyance. That seemed an inordinate time to waste on such a frill. But the Ghayrog was quite particular about his craft.

"And what good will all this pretty lettering do, anyway?" Harpirias demanded of Korinaam when the finished copies were at last brought to him. "The king can't read a single word of Majipoori. What's written here isn't going to seem any more important to him than bird-scratchings in the snow. Shouldn't we at least have drawn up a copy of it in Othinor also?"

"There is no written Othinor language," Korinaam observed, a trifle smugly.

"None at all?"

"Have you seen many books in your wanderings through the village, prince?"

Harpirias flushed. "Even so—a treaty that can't be read by one of the signatories—doesn't that seem awfully unilateral to you, Korinaam?"

The Shapeshifter gave Harpirias what might have been a malicious look. He had recovered much of his aplomb in the time that had passed since his performance in the high country; but some residue of resentment for what Harpirias had forced him to do unmistakably remained.

"Ah, prince, have no fear! The king will admire and respect the copy that we give him! He'll hang it on his throne-room wall and stroke it fondly from time to time, and why should it matter whether he can read it or not? All that really concerns you—is it not so?—is getting the hostages back; and that much has been agreed upon. Once you have them and have left this place behind you, what further value does the treaty have, to you or to the king?"

"To me, none. But presumably it has some for the king. It gives him, after all, the thing he most wishes, which is protection for the people of this valley against further incursions by the forces of the government of Majipoor."

"Yes. That is surely true." Korinaam laughed harshly.

"What bold soul would dare defy the sacred clauses of this treaty? If at some time in years to come a future Coronal should be so venturesome as to send an army in here, why, whoever occupies Toikella's throne at that time will simply need to take the treaty down from the wall and wave it in the face of the commanding officer of the invading force, and that officer will immediately order his troops to withdraw! Is that not so, prince? For that has always been the way the people of Majipoor treat those who have less power than they. Tell me, prince: is that not so?"

Harpirias let the Shapeshifter's heavy sarcasm pass. Undoubtedly Korinaam had his own Piurivar axes to grind; but Harpirias had no desire to fight Lord Stiamot's war all over again ten thousand years later. Whatever unpleasantnesses the human settlers of Majipoor had imposed on Korinaam's ancestors long ago were ancient history now, and had been atoned for, insofar as atonement for the taking of a world was possible at all, by the reconciliation of the races that had begun in the time of Valentine Pontifex. Whatever grievances Korinaam persisted in holding were no affair of Harpirias's. Finishing this business with the Othinor was all that interested him now.

He studied the parchment. It was, he had to admit, very nicely lettered indeed. As for the text, he was quite proud of it: crisp in style, efficient and straightforward in setting forth the obligations of the respective signatory parties. No ambiguities or equivocations so far as he could tell, nothing that could be misconstrued or misinterpreted. The Coronal Lord of Majipoor agreed to respect the sovereignty of His Royal Highness the King of the Othinor, and to avoid any further unwanted incursions upon his domain, the king's domain being defined as beginning at such-and-such a parallel of north latitude on the continent of Zimroel and extending to the planetary pole, et cetera, et cetera. For his part, His Highness the King of the Othinor undertook immediately to release from custody the nine paleontologists who had accidentally intruded upon the sovereign territory of the Kingdom of the Othinor, and to return to them such scientific specimens as they had collected, et cetera, et cetera.

Nothing was said about continued paleontological research in this area. The king almost certainly would have boggled at that, considering that the main thing he wanted from this treaty was a promise that he would never be troubled by contact with Majipoori citizens again. The scientists, once they were freed, could always petition the Coronal to negotiate an agreement with Toikella permitting them to resume their exploration in Othinor territory. But Harpirias hoped that some ambassador other than himself would be the one who got the job of negotiating that agreement.

Nor was there any clause covering repatriation to the civilized parts of Majipoor of the children that had been born of Majipoor fathers and Othinor mothers. Best not to touch on that subject at all, Harpirias thought, though he did feel some private discomfort about it. The children would be Othinor, and that was that.

" '*And so,*' " he read, coming to the bottom of the sheet, " '*we the Coronal Lord Ambinole herewith signify our approval and solemnly make our royal pledge—*' "

Harpirias looked up from his reading.

"Wait a minute," he said. "The way it's worded here, the signature of the Coronal himself is called for. That's not what I—"

"I asked the Ghayrog to make a slight change," said Korinaam blandly.

"You did *what?*"

"King Toikella has never grasped the fact that you are merely an ambassador. He continues to believe that he has been host to the person of Lord Ambinole."

"But I told you a thousand times to let him know that—"

"I appreciate your concern, prince. Nevertheless, at this point the primary object, is it not, is to maintain the cooperation of the king until the hostages are freed and we have safely withdrawn from his territory? At this stage of things the king can only react badly to the revelation of your true identity. Even now, with the treaty completely negotiated and ready for signing, such a revelation might have explosive effects."

"I'll give him explosive effects!" Harpirias exclaimed. "He's seen what our energy-throwers can do. If he refuses to release those men, after all the talking that's gone on here—"

"You can order your soldiers to do great damage, oh, yes, certainly. But I remind you that the hostages remain in his custody to this moment. If he has them put to death, even while your troops are demonstrating the power of their energy-throwers—what have you accomplished then, prince? Sign the document with the name of Lord Ambinole, I implore you."

"I will not. I draw the line at fraud."

"Fraud is a very small sin. I call it to your attention once more that our main purpose—"

"Is the release of the hostages. Right. But what happens when the signed text of the treaty reaches Castle Mount? What will the Coronal say, when he sees that I've forged his name? No, no, Korinaam. I'll sign as Harpirias of Muldemar. As you've already pointed out, King Toikella can't read anyway. Let him interpret the signature any way he wants."

Which was where the discussion ended; for at that moment a messenger from the king arrived, bearing word that the grand feast of celebration, at which the treaty would be formally signed and the hostages brought forth, was ready to begin in the royal banqueting hall.

It seemed to Harpirias that a great many months had gone by since that other grand feast in the royal hall, the one on his first night here, welcoming him to the land of the Othinor. But he knew it could not be nearly that long a time: some number of weeks, yes, but surely not months. The sky these days still remained light far into the evening and the heavy snows of winter had not yet begun. Yet he could understand now why the hostages had lost track of time here, had even forgotten what year it was. In this valley one day faded imperceptibly into the next. Twoday, Threeday, Seaday, Starday, who could tell which was which? There were no calendars here. The only clock was the clock of the heavens: the sun, the stars, the moons.

In the feasting hall everything was exactly as it had been that other time. The heavy white rugs of steetmoy fur had been unpacked and spread on the floor; the great tables of rough planks laid over trestles made of hajbarak bones had been assembled; the innumerable bowls and plates and tureens brimming with food had been set out. The king was on his high throne and an assortment of his wives and daughters lounged at its base.

Everything was the same, yes. In the intervening weeks only Harpirias had changed; for now the dense, smoky air of the great room seemed perfectly natural to him, and the odors rising from the dishes of food, rather than rousing uneasiness in the pit of his stomach, actually stirred his appetite, for he had grown accustomed to the dry stringy meats and fiery sauces of these people, to their baked roots and roasted nuts, their bitter beer, their acrid, glutinous soups and stews. The dissonant screeing and skirling of the king's musicians was familiar to him now also, and when occasionally some bawdy words would drift to him out of the group of Othinor warriors standing against the side wall, he would sometimes grin with comprehension, for in the course of his nights with Ivla Yevikenik he had learned more than a little of the Othinor language.

The dancing before the meal was very much the same as before, too: the wives of the king, first, and then a ponderous solo for Toikella himself, and then Harpirias invited to join him on the floor. This time, though, Harpirias called Ivla Yevikenik out of the group of royal princesses to accompany him. The girl's eyes gleamed with pleasure as she came forward to dance with him; and Toikella too, in his own dark and somber way, appeared pleased at the honor being paid his daughter.

After the dancing came the dining, and along with it the drinking, round upon round of formal toasting in long, orotund outbursts of Othinor oratory. Harpirias was skilled enough in the ways of high ceremonial dinners on Castle Mount to understand the art of keeping his consumption of the potent Othinor beer as low as was diplomatically permissible: a sip where the others took a gulp, all the while pretending to be swilling the stuff down as lustily as everybody else. The wisdom of that tactic was confirmed when the beer mugs were cleared away and two bowls of finely polished stone were ostentatiously laid out on a long narrow table that had been set up at the foot of the throne. A high official of the court now entered, bearing a tall alabaster vessel, from which he carefully poured into each of the bowls a clear, bright fluid: a brandy or liqueur of some sort, evidently.

Sounds of awe and surprise could be heard around the room. Harpirias guessed that this must be some very special beverage indeed, something consumed only on the most momentous of ceremonial occasions: the coronation of a king, say, or the birth of a royal heir. Or the consummation of a treaty with a fellow monarch, Harpirias supposed.

Slowly and majestically Toikella descended from his throne, walked to the table that held the bowls, picked one of them up in both his hands. The king looked strangely grim and tense. All this evening the king had seemed uncharacteristically bleak and edgy and withdrawn, even during the dancing, even during the noisiest part of the feasting; but now his expression was positively funereal. Which was very much out of keeping with the presumable joyousness of the moment.

What was bothering him? What had become of his natural exuberance, his colossal profligate vitality?

He stared across at Harpirias, then at the bowl that remained at the table. The meaning was clear enough; Harpirias rose, went to the table, lifted his bowl in both hands as Toikella had done. Then he waited. Toikella's great bulk loomed oppressively over him. Harpirias felt dwarfed by the king, disturbingly overshadowed. And the king's black glare bothered him most of all.

Was there poison in his bowl? Was that why Toikella had turned so edgy as he waited for Harpirias to take the fatal draught?

But that was nonsense, Harpirias knew. Both bowls had been filled from the same vessel. Toikella would not be planning a joint suicide as the climax of this evening's festivities.

The king raised his bowl to his lips. Harpirias did the same. For a moment the king's eyes met those of Harpirias across the rim of the bowl: they had a baleful look, a look of barely contained anger. Something is very wrong here, Harpirias thought. He glanced over uncertainly at Ivla Yevikenik. She smiled and nodded; she mimed lifting the bowl and drinking. Would *she* betray him? No. No. The bowl must be safe.

He took a tentative sip.

The stuff was like liquid fire. Harpirias felt it burning a track to the bottom of his gut. He gasped, steeled himself, cautiously took a second sip. Toikella had already drained his bowl: no doubt he was expected to do likewise. The second jolt was easier. Already Harpirias could feel his head beginning to swim a little. Much still remained in the bowl. Would it be a dire loss of face if he failed to drink it all down? He was the personal representative of the Coronal, after all. In Toikella's eyes he *was* the Coronal. He could not allow himself to disgrace the honor of Majipoor before these barbarians.

He gulped and gulped again, and a third gulp gave him the last of the brandy. It hit with a frightful impact. His shoulders quivered violently, almost convulsively. His head throbbed and whirled. For a moment he swayed and thought he would fall;

but then he steadied himself and planted his feet firmly on the floor.

By the Lady, would the king fill those bowls again?

No, he would not. The Divine be thanked, Toikella was content with a single draught of the stuff!

"Treaty," the king said gruffly. He still looked grim. "Now we sign."

"Yes," said Harpirias. He fought back another shiver, another wobble. "Now we sign."

The two parchment scrolls were produced and arrayed side by side on the table before the throne. A chair made of bone was brought for the king, and another for Harpirias, and they too sat side by side, looking out at the assembled grandees of the Othinor. Korinaam stood just behind Harpirias in his role as interpreter and adviser, and Mankhelm took up the same position in back of the king.

Toikella, seizing one scroll in his immense paws and holding it high, scrutinized it line by line as though he could actually read it; then, with a grunt, he put it down, picked up the other copy, and began to give it the same survey. Harpirias noted with some satisfaction that the king was reading this one upside down.

"Everything good?" Harpirias asked him.

"Everything good, yes. We sign."

Korinaam handed Harpirias a stylus that had already been

inked. The Shapeshifter leaned forward and said, in a low cutting voice, "You see the place where you must sign, do you not, your lordship?"

"I have no intention of signing the name of—"

"Sign, lordship. Quickly. You must. There is no alternative."

In quick angry strokes Harpirias wrote in at the bottom of the scroll the name that was required of him there: *Ambinole Coronal Lord.* It seemed monstrous to him, almost blasphemous. He stared at the fraudulent signature for an instant; and then, before Korinaam could object, he added underneath, *Harpirias of Muldemar, on Lord Ambinole's behalf.* Let King Toikella make of that whatever he would—or could.

He gave the signed scroll to the king, and received the other in return. Toikella had painstakingly inscribed a bold, jagged, illiterate scribble in the lower left corner. Opposite it Harpirias once more wrote the Coronal's name, and once more added his own beneath.

It was done. The treaty was signed.

"Goszmar," Harpirias said. "The hostages, now."

"Goszmar," Toikella grunted, nodding brusquely. And signaled; and the feasting-hall door was thrown open, and the nine prisoners of the ice-cave came marching uncertainly in, the wild-eyed figure of Salvinor Hesz leading the group.

He rushed to Harpirias and fell to his knees. "Are we really free?"

Harpirias indicated the two scrolls before him on the table. "Everything's signed and sealed. We'll leave here first thing in the morning."

"Free! Free at last! And the fossils—I saw them sitting outside the hall, prince, the whole collection! Will they be returned also?"

"The Othinor will provide porters to carry them to the floaters that we have parked outside the village," Harpirias said.

"Free! Free! Can it really be?" In a desperate frenzy the paleontologists embraced one another. Some seemed almost manic with glee; some seemed to be having trouble believing that their captivity was ending.

Harpirias said, "Give these men meat and drink. This is their celebration too!"

Toikella acceded with a surly wave of his hand. More beer was poured; more platters of meat were brought. But Harpirias saw that the king had drawn aside and stood sulkily watching, taking no part in the festivity.

Was Toikella planning some treachery as the culmination of the feast? Did that account for his strange brooding mood, for the air of tension that had surrounded him all evening?

Harpirias said quietly to Ivla Yevikenik, "Your father—what troubles him tonight?"

The girl hesitated. He could see her searching for words. "Nothing troubles him tonight," she said finally.

"He is not like himself."

"He is tired. He is—yes, that is it. He is tired."

She made hardly any effort at all to sound convincing.

"No," Harpirias said. He stared angrily at his fingertips and cursed the limitations of his Othinor vocabulary. Then, looking intensely into her eyes, he said, "Tell me the truth, Ivla Yevikenik. Something is bad here. What is it?"

"He is—afraid."

"Afraid? *Him?* Of what?"

A long pause. Then: "You. Your people. Your weapons."

"He shouldn't be. There's a treaty now. We guarantee the safety and freedom of the Othinor."

"You *guarantee* it, yes," the girl said. And the bitter inflection of her tone explained everything to Harpirias.

Indeed the king was frightened. And angry and humiliated; and these were all new emotions for him. Toikella had learned at last what sort of antagonist he was really up against, and the knowledge had thrown him into an anguish beyond all bearing.

Perhaps Ivla Yevikenik had passed along to her father some of Harpirias's descriptions of the greatness and splendor of Majipoor, his tales of the richness of its superabundant crops and the wealth of its swift rivers, the myriads of its people, the two mighty continents studded with innumerable huge cities, and above all else the serene grandeur of Castle Mount and the immensity of the royal dwelling-place at its summit. Whatever she had understood of his stories—magnified, very likely, by the distortions and enhancements of her own free-ranging imagination, so that the genuinely magnificent was transformed into the inconceivably awesome—was probably what Ivla Yevikenik had poured into Toikella's reeling mind.

And then the sight of the energy-throwers in action—those rugged stone crags disintegrating under the force of the purple light that came from the metal tubes in the hands of Harpirias's little army—the hated Eililylal fleeing like vermin as the rocks came tumbling down—

Small wonder that the king's mood was dark. For the first time in his life he found himself up against a force that could never be made to yield to his booming and his blustering. He was coming to understand the truth about the world: that his little kingdom would have no hope of being able to stand against the power of the vast unknown realm that lay somewhere beyond his snowy borders. He had begun the process of discovering that the mighty King Toikella was nothing more than a flea on the backside of Majipoor; and that process hurt. Oh, how it must hurt!

Harpirias realized that he felt genuinely sorry for the fierce old monster—that in fact he had actually come to like Toikella, and had had no wish to be the cause of his undoing.

He looked around for Korinaam, and called him to his side. What he needed to say was too delicate to attempt in his own clumsy and erratic Othinor.

"I want you to let him know," he told the Shapeshifter,

"that we of Majipoor will regard the treaty that we have just signed as a sacred obligation: that its terms will safeguard the independence of the Othinor forever."

"He knows these things already," said Korinaam.

"Never mind what he may or may not know already. Tell him. Tell him to have faith in the treaty, and in me. Tell him that his people will never come to harm at our hands."

"As you wish, prince."

Korinaam turned to the king and spoke at length; and so far as Harpirias could tell the Shapeshifter was accurately rendering the things he had been told to say. But that only appeared to make matters worse. Toikella's frown deepened; the king chewed at his lower lip and balled his fists and rammed his great knobby knuckles together until they popped; his nostrils flared, his cheeks went taut with mounting displeasure.

When he made his reply, Toikella looked not at Korinaam but at Harpirias, and his response was brief and sardonic in tone, edged with unmistakable ferocity:

"I give you my thanks. I am grateful for your mercy."

Harpirias had no difficulty in understanding the king's words, or the meaning that they carried beneath their surface. Toikella fully recognized that his power would continue only by sufferance of the lords of Majipoor; and that was not an easy thing for him to accept.

Still Harpirias felt the need to offer some expression of sympathy and reassurance.

"Your majesty—my good royal friend—"

Toikella replied with a growl. "Go, now. Go, leave this room, leave this land. And may none of you ever return to this place—you, or any of your kind."

Korinaam volunteered a translation. But Harpirias waved him to silence. He had no doubt of the meaning of what the king had said.

Harpirias held out his hand to him. Toikella peered at it as though it were a soiled thing. An icy aura of offended royal dignity, as chilly as the darkest day of the Othinor winter, emanated from him.

"We are not afraid," Toikella said loftily. "Let the empire do its worst—we will be ready. Even if you send an army of two hundred men against us! *Three* hundred!"

There was nothing Harpirias could say in return. Best to leave things as they were, he thought. Toikella's pride, at least, was still intact. And perhaps the wounds of this visit would heal after a while, and in his old age he would boast of how he had forced the Coronal of Majipoor to come crawling to him once upon a time to gain the release of his explorers, and how he had extracted from the Coronal a child of royal blood in payment for the hostages he had taken.

So be it, Harpirias thought. Korinaam had been right after all: nothing would have been gained by forcing the truth down Toikella's throat, and much would have been lost.

He bade the king a formal farewell, which Toikella received stonily, with great hauteur; and then he turned to Ivla Yevikenik for one last fond and weepy moment with his Othinor princess. But what could he say to her? What, indeed, could he say? For all his Castle Mount eloquence, nothing came to him now. She stared solemnly at him; he smiled; she managed a smile of sorts as well; her tears glistened; she blotted them with the back of her hand. He could not kiss her goodbye. Kissing was not the custom here. In the end Harpirias took her hand and held it a time, and let it go. She took his, and put it lightly to her belly, and kept it captive there for a moment, resting on her, as though to let him feel the new life that was quickening there. Then she released him and turned away.

Harpirias gathered his troops and beckoned to the freed hostages to follow him, and went out of the feasting-hall.

18

From the look of the star-speckled darkness overhead, dawn was still some hours off. But it took the rest of the night to load the waiting floaters and make them ready for the homeward journey. The sky was already streaked with pink before all the final tasks were finished.

Harpirias stood for a moment just outside the high wall of stone that surrounded the hidden kingdom of the Othinor.

Home, now! Home to the waiting warmth of civilized Majipoor—and, perhaps, the resurrection of his own interrupted career on Castle Mount. He had actually accomplished the task he had been sent here to do; more than that, he had had his great adventure and he had gained a lifetime's worth of stories to tell, stories that the Coronal would listen to eagerly, and everyone else as well. And now home to tell those stories; home to a decent bath, and a dinner of real food, oysters and spiced fish and breast of sekkimaund or haunch of bilantoon, and the thick strong wine of Muldemar or the bright crimson wine of Bannikanniklole or the golden wine of Piliplok or the fine silvery-gray wine of Amblemorn, maybe all four in quick succession—with some clear-eyed beauty with high cheekbones and delicate brows as his companion for the night, yes, or—why not?—two or three—

But Harpirias knew that the land of the Othinor had imprinted itself upon his soul forever. Beyond any doubt he would dream time and again of the land of the Othinor, when finally he was home once more. Images of the ice-world would steal into his mind, and of King Toikella's smoky banquet-hall, and of the jeering, capering Eililylal of the heights: that he knew. And the glossy-haired girl with a sliver of carved bone through her upper lip who had slipped into his room to keep him warm on so many frosty nights: she too would come to him in his sleep.

Yes. Yes. All that and much more: Harpirias was certain of that. He would never forget this place.

"Everything is stowed, prince," Eskenazo Marabaud called to him. "Sun's about to come up. Shall we get going?"

"In a moment," Harpirias said.

He stepped back through the narrow wedge-shaped crack in the mountain wall that afforded the only access to King Toikella's land. The ice-village gleamed faintly in the pearly light of dawn. Harpirias let his eyes rove the shining fanciful facades, the glittering icy filigrees.

A small figure was standing in front of the lodge where his

quarters had been. At this distance, it was hard for him to see her clearly, but Harpirias could envision her well enough in the eye of his mind, a ragged smudgy figure in carelessly arrayed furs, a girl who perhaps was bearing his Othinor child. Waving to him, hesitantly at first, then more eagerly, a gesture of obvious love and longing.

He stared at her for a time. Then he waved back at her, and turned and walked away, passing through the crevice in the mountain wall and heading for his floater to begin his long journey home.